VET AMONG THE PIGEONS

A Star Original

Fifth in the remarkably funny series by the author of *It's a Vet's Life, The Vet Has Nine Lives, Vets in the Belfry* and *Vets in Congress*.

When Michael Morton does his yearly stint as a locum for his friend Phil Brogan in the less than idyllic village of Craftly, trouble, unsurprisingly, comes his way. Tiger and Claire have gone into the livestock business, and have a herd of sheep, headed by a magnificent ewe nicknamed the Bionic Baa. But the omnipresent Ministry of Agriculture, trying to combat an unpleasant disease of sheep, demands that they use a sheep dip so virulent that it threatens to be more destructive than the disease itself. Michael Morton, of course, takes on the blinkered bureaucracy with crusading fervour – and hilarious consequences.

D1331755

Also by Alex Duncan in *Star:*

IT'S A VET'S LIFE
THE VET HAS NINE LIVES
VETS IN THE BELFRY
VETS IN CONGRESS

VET AMONG
THE PIGEONS

Alex Duncan

A STAR BOOK

published by

the Paperback Division of

W. H. ALLEN & Co. Ltd.

A Star Book
Published in 1977
by the Paperback Division of
W. H. Allen & Co. Ltd.
A Howard & Wyndham Company
44 Hill Street, London W1X 8LB

Copyright © 1977 by Alex Duncan

Printed in Great Britain by
Richard Clay (The Chaucer Press) Ltd., Bungay, Suffolk

ISBN 0 352 39569 9

CHAPTER 1

'Don't know what to make of it,' said Colonel Hanley. 'I mean, this business of people getting poisoned because the farmers are bathing their sheep in some sort of chemical dip. It's beyond an ordinary chap like me.'

Colonel Hanley, my father-in-law, was lying flat on his back on the stone kitchen floor, a whisky at his fingertips. He was wearing black cotton trousers and a matching kimono with white Japanese characters embroidered down the front. Though his face was ruddy and his hair cut short he looked anything but an *ordinary* chap.

'Daddy, do get up,' said Julia. 'You're upsetting Mike.'

'Poppycock. Your son's a sensible chap. Matter of fact he's getting on pretty well with his yoga.'

'Oh daddy!' wailed Julia. 'Why can't you teach him something . . . something more English?'

It occurred to me that I'd had a damping effect on my wife. Before we'd been married she wouldn't have blinked an eyelid at her father's behaviour. She wouldn't even have noticed him lying on the kitchen floor in a Japanese outfit. Nor would she have demurred at his teaching an eight-year-old – let alone our Mike – yoga. Now, in the middle of cooking the Colonel a curry, she was feeling vaguely embarrassed.

'Daddy, do go and sit on a chair.'

'Don't be silly, girl. In this damned heat it's much cooler on the floor . . . As I was saying, that chap in the pub was ranting on about the sheep-dip killing the lot of us.' The colonel lifted his head. 'I say . . . you don't think it's the sheep-dip that's given Biddy the collywobbles, do you?'

'How can it be?' I asked him. 'You only arrived a couple of hours ago. Biddy was sick before you came; not here.'

'Fair enough, old man, fair enough.' Still on the floor,

1

Colonel Hanley watched his daughter pick up a heavy tray of plates and cutlery. Before I could help Julia, she'd pushed open the door with her shoulder. 'She's splendid, isn't she?'

I thought so too. My Julia was no slouch. While I was doing a locum for Phil Brogan, running his veterinary practice in the country, Julia was supposed to be having a holiday from running a home. But when I'd offered to take the family out to dinner she'd refused. Why shouldn't she cook a meal on Mrs Cockman's evening off? It was great letting Phil's housekeeper do all the work, but it was fun to have the kitchen to herself once in a while. Besides, no one else could make a curry just as daddy liked it.

Through the glass doors between kitchen and yard – or *patio,* as Phil would have it – I could see Julia fold the table napkins into sailing boats. Eating out of doors was a pleasure we couldn't have in London. Suddenly it seemed a good idea that I'd agreed to spending my holiday doing Phil's work at Craftly while he was living it up in the South of France. Julia, in a floating white hostess dress, her black hair streaming down her back, looked marvellous against the background of the harvested golden fields and the mellow old village.

Phil's house on the hill overlooked one of the most attractive views of farmland Surrey I knew. Not a whiff of suburbia anywhere. Had I known Craftly sooner, I'd never have taken over Uncle Simon's Knightsbridge practice. At heart I was a countryman. Or was I? Had I ever been mad about a cow with brucellosis aborting in the middle of a freezing night? No, to be perfectly honest I was not brilliant at handling sick cows or sheep; I felt more at home with the dogs and cats at my London practice.

'Michael . . .' My father-in-law had shifted his position on the floor. He ran a long hand over his bald patch. 'You know – between you and me – I don't think my girl's altogether happy.'

'Unhappy?' Was the Colonel, with his long experience of the mysterious East, sensing something that I couldn't? Yet

2

Julia couldn't have looked more contented, out there in the evening sun, watching young Mike play with her father's black alsatian. Nothing she liked better than a visit from her dad and making a curry for him – always provided that the Colonel and his dog returned to Leamington Spa after one weekend. They were too much alike to enjoy one another's company, except in small doses.

I said, 'She's fine. You're imagining things.'

Father-in-law looked at me, grey eyes as clear and frank as Julia's. 'I'm telling you, my boy . . . she's far from happy. And I don't care how much she's prancing around.'

'Well, what do you think's the matter?'

'That's something I'd expect *you* to know. Haven't you noticed the way she keeps her head down? You take my word for it Michael . . . I know the bitch.'

'I wish you wouldn't call . . .'

'Why ever not? I believe in calling a spade a spade. And I can tell you, I've never known a bitch like her. Got to watch her all the time or . . .'

'You're being most unfair.' I couldn't make out what my father-in-law was driving at. Sure, he'd always been eccentric. But even in his Japanese kimono, flat on the stone floor, he had a certain dignity. And he'd never been a mischief-maker. Yet, with advancing age, some people changed. 'Colonel, I wish you'd come straight out with it.'

'Haven't I made myself clear?' he asked mildly. 'I'm sorry Michael. Look here . . . I know she's a fine bitch. I'm not denying it. But if I didn't know that it's the wrong time, I'd say she wants to be out on the tiles.'

'Surely Julia and I are the best judges . . .'

'The abnormal weather might have something to do with it,' continued the Colonel, unperturbed. 'I mean to say . . . here we are in autumn and the heat's almost as bad as it used to be in Delhi . . . in the old days, before they sent us the electric fans. Kind of thing that might upset any bitch . . .'

'Will you please stop calling my wife a bitch!'

'Your wife?' Colonel Hanley blinked. He looked a little hurt. 'My boy, never call a woman a bitch. *I* never did, I assure you . . . though Julia's mother wasn't always the easiest lady to live with. Artistic temperament, don't you know. Not a bad painter as a matter of fact. Wouldn't part with that picture of a tiger for anything in the world. Won't even give it to Julia until I'm dead . . . But let's face it, old man, she *is* a bitch. Fact, plain fact. I know, you vets are a funny lot but surely even you wouldn't want me to call my alsatian a *lady dog*. Now, would you?

Knowing Biddy, father-in-law's black alsatian, I was not surprised that we had a disturbed night. Normally Biddy had a strong sense of duty and of priorities. On arrival in Craftly she'd carried out a survey of our temporary home and examined gardens, grounds and Phil's surgery. That chore completed, she'd taken up a position on the patio – the best vantage point – and barked somewhat tentatively at the distant passers-by. The colonel assured us that Biddy would soon learn *the drill* – who to welcome and who to bark at. By the time Julia had served the curry Biddy had in fact settled down; she was sitting upright beside her owner, attention focused on the dinner table, nose twitching. The colonel had assured me often enough that no animal of his was allowed to beg at table. Biddy didn't exactly beg; she just grudged us every mouthful until Julia, Mike and I carelessly dropped bits of meat and rice. The food gone, Biddy had gone to sleep and that should have been the end of her Saturday.

But, as the colonel had observed, Biddy wasn't herself. Or perhaps she was, because she'd always considered sex and motherhood her chief function in life. All night long, on and off, I heard her big paws tick along the stairs and corridors and by morning she'd disappeared.

'I knew it,' the colonel told us at breakfast. 'Just like a woman,' he added, philosophically.

'Daddy, aren't you going to look for Biddy?' asked Julia.

'Don't be silly, girl. He smiled at Mrs Cockman, who was serving him a second helping of bacon and eggs. 'Ruin a capital breakfast? Not likely.'

4

I said, 'Your Biddy might be chasing sheep. This isn't Leamington Spa.'

'Neither it is, my boy, neither it is.'

'Well then . . . hadn't you better . . .'

'Don't rush me, Michael. No point.'

'Daddy,' Mike wriggled in his chair, 'may I get down?'

'If you've finished your breakfast.'

Mike crammed the last of his toast into his mouth and made for the door.

'Where are you going?'

'Manor house.'

'You're not to go near the pond,' I told him.

'Don't want to go to the pond, Daddy. We're going to work on the project.'

I knew that determined look on my child's face. 'What project, Mike?'

'Dad!' he rebuked. 'Have you forgotten? The multi-ethnic project, of course.'

Multi-ethnic it was, in our boy's view, because he was co-operating with the children of the Arab who had bought the manor house. 'Ah yes,' I remembered. 'Beetles, isn't it?'

'What beetles?' Mike tested me.

'*Drosophilidae*..'

'That was the project we did at school,' Mike said disgustedly.

'That's right, darling,' chipped in Julia. 'It's *Phyllotreta* the Habib boys and Mike are working on now.'

'S'right mum.' Mike was pacified. 'Don't wait for me . . . I suppose I'll have lunch at the manor.'

Julia and I looked at one another, taken aback – not for the first time – by the self-possession of the small figure in jeans and T-shirt. To me it seemed that our Mike was already headed for the presidency of the British Veterinary Association.

'Hang on!' Julia stopped Mike. 'Perhaps your grandfather would like to go along with you . . . to look for Biddy.'

'He won't,' stated Mike. 'Byeee.'

'Bright little chap,' said the colonel. 'Got more sense than his mother, don't you know. No point chasing after Biddy. She'll come back when she's had what she wants. Pity she didn't wait for a mate of her own breed . . . though I must admit she's got good taste. Those half-labrador pups of hers weren't bad, not bad at all. Wonder what she'll produce this time.'

The last thing I expected was an answer to my father-in-law's rhetorical question. Yet it came . . . Biddy and a fine looking Scotch collie walking across the lawn to the house as quietly as a bridal pair approaching the altar. They were accompanied by a tall red-haired and bearded man with a shot-gun under his arm – Viscount St George Clemens, *Tiger* to Julia and me.

'Good God!' exclaimed the colonel.

'It's all right, Daddy,' Julia assured him. 'Tiger doesn't really go around shooting things. Actually he's a playwright.'

'I'll be damned! Fellows like that shouldn't play around with guns . . . not even with these little sporting jobs. Matter of fact, *he* is the chap I met in the pub . . . fellow who was ranting on about chemicals in the sheep-dip killing people. Anything in it?'

CHAPTER 2

On the hot September Sunday morning Craftly was all churchbells and peace. And Tiger, dressed in white trousers and a lilac shirt, added to the illusion that we were holiday-makers in a semi-tropical country. The second crop of wisteria flowers on the sixteenth-century brick wall; Julia and her father, in garden chairs under the blue awning, reading the Sunday papers; Biddy and her new mate playing on the lawn.

Mrs Cockman had brought us a jug of iced lemonade and Tiger, as usual, had drained his glass without noticing what he was drinking. The weeks of continuous sunshine had bleached his ginger hair and increased his freckles, making him look more like a schoolboy than a famous playwright in his thirties.

'Bachelor's absolutely super,' he told me.

'Who is?'

'My collie. His proper name's Bachelor of Dunwoody. First rate working sheepdog. His pups are worth having.'

'My father-in-law's accepted the inevitable.' I refilled Tiger's glass. 'Your Siamese cats can't be too pleased with the dog.'

'They don't see much of Bachelor. He spends most of his time out of doors and with my livestock manager.'

'I didn't know you went in for livestock, Tiger.'

'Sheep; that's all. Matter of fact it all began when Dave Thornton gave us a new-born lamb. Its mother had died and it didn't look too promising either. Claire nursed and bottled-fed the thing . . . well, you know her. We finished up with a great big sheep . . . such a whopper that Claire called her Bionic Baa and got worried about her sex life. So Dave Thornton obliged us with a suitable ram and Bionic Baa became the founder of our flock. Last year we formed a new company – Baa-sis Ltd. Actually it was Claire's idea . . . she's got the business head. My play *Three Corsets to Curzon Street* was on Broadway, going like a bomb, and the tax people were stripping us. Claire said we needed a company that makes a loss – I have no idea how it works – and Baa-sis Ltd does seem to cost a mint.'

'But you pay less income tax?'

'Remains to be seen. Thing is, we've given Willard and his man the cottage – free, of course. And there's the wages . . . for the two of them. Of course, Willard's a horse-man . . . useless with a flock. It's Masters who knows all there is to know about sheep.'

Ever since I'd met Tiger and Claire in London, some ten years ago, I'd liked them and I'd taken it for granted that I'd never understand what they were talking about. Tiger's surrealist plays such as *Three Brassieres to Bond Street* and Claire's passion for lilac colours and lilac-pointed Siamese cats had always been as incomprehensible to me as their diet of deep-frozen foods and their conversation about people I'd never heard of. Now, for the first time, I was beginning to feel that Tiger and I were on the same wavelength at last.

'Are you talking of the Duke of Alanspring and his butler?' I asked, hopefully.

'Well . . . yes. I'd better fill you in . . .'

I remembered my beginnings as a vet and one of my earliest patients – Grey Rainbow, the Duke of Alanspring's greyhound. He'd been a perfect specimen except that he'd been allergic to hares and rabbits. The duke, impoverished as he was, had never given up his hopes of racing the dog and his butler, Masters, had been too loyal to disillusion him. Somehow the two of them scraped together enough money to take Grey Rainbow to a dog psychiatrist in the States.

Next, I'd met the trio in New York. Grey Rainbow had still been allergic to hares and even to gloves lined with rabbit-fur. At the mere sight of a rabbit-skin coat the dog had shivered, slunk into a dark corner and sneezed his head off. Yet the duke had made a success of the trip. He'd married Sonia, the widow of millionaire Egon Miller-Hundling, and was about to start a business in California – the most luxurious kennels in the world.

'It broke up,' said Tiger, sadly.

'The duke's marriage?'

'Yes . . . well, actually it wasn't his fault. Perhaps if he hadn't been so civilized about it . . . You remember the chap Sonia got to advise on animal training? Abdul Karim Kochbar . . . Rugby and Oxford . . .'

'Indian who ran the Self-Knowledge Temple and employed executive priestesses to perform the *mysteries*?'

'Right. Well, Sonia got hooked on him and divorced poor old Willard. Still calls herself *duchess* though. Anyway she married Abdul.'

'I thought that Indian philosopher didn't believe in marriage.'

'He's given up philosophy and is running Sonia's kennels . . . concentrating on the animal training side. It was rather tough on poor old Willard. When he got back from the States he was as broke as ever.'

'So you made him your livestock manager.'

'Yes . . . well, Masters takes care of the sheep. But Willard is frightfully good with our cats. Since he and Masters have been in the cottage we can go abroad at a moment's notice . . . knowing that Min and Chiang-Ch'ing will be all right. It's a relief.'

'And the collie?'

'Willard's job, that goes without saying. He is a dog man, basically.'

'Well, I expect we'll be seeing him before we go back to London.'

'You will. But above all you'll have to get together with Masters. Absolutely vital.'

There it was. I'd almost certainly put my head in a noose once again. And judging by the urgency in Tiger's voice I'd soon be learning something about the nature of the noose.

'Look here Michael . . . I simply can't deal with it myself. No time. I'm in the middle of rehearsing *Psht* . . .'

'Your new play?'

'Right. *Psht* is frightfully demanding . . . more than any other play I've done. You see, we have this problem of putting over the *idea* of one half of the world not communicating with the other half because the tools – words, that is – have become meaningless and therefore useless . . .'

'Tiger, you're using words right now and I understand . . . or I think I understand . . . what you're saying.'

'Ah, but you're not sure, are you? That's why – for the first time ever – I haven't *written* the play. I'm devising it, y'see. And that means I've got to put in all the hard work at the producing stage. No script to work on; just graphs . . . you know, the sort of up-and-down squiggles government departments put in their reports when inflation goes through the roof . . . and when they're trying to brainwash us into believing that prices aren't going up as fast as we *know* they are. You with me Michael?'

'More or less.'

'Right. Claire and I will be working on *Psht* until Christmas. That's when the play's opening. So it'll be up to my livestock manager and his man to give you a hand with the problem. Are you with me?'

'No.'

'Oh, well . . . never mind. I've brought you all the correspondence and the literature. Claire says you're definitely the man to deal with it.'

'Deal with what?'

Tiger dumped a thick file on the table and gave a shrill whistle, His collie, abandoning father-in-law's alsatian, went to his heel. 'It's all here, Michael, We've got to prevent them from destroying our kidneys.'

'Prevent whom, Tiger?'

'The men from the ministry of course. Got to get back for lunch now. Claire's making game paté.'

Father-in-law lifted his head from the newspaper. 'Got game on your land, have you?'

'No, 'fraid not.' Tiger picked up his gun. 'The paté's out

of the freezer. New thing they're selling at the Key Market. The picture on the packet looks super. First time we've seen frozen stuff from Mogadiscio.'

I couldn't believe it. 'From where?'

'Place in East Africa.'

'I suppose you know what's in the paté?'

'Claire always looks at the small print before she buys a packet . . . though we're not sure what Dick-Dick is.'

'A very small African gazelle,' I told him.

'I say . . . that's rather a shame. Still, I suppose it's no worse than putting rabbits in a stew. Anyway, the other contents seem pretty straight forward . . . stuff like monosodium glutamate. It's in a lot of tins and packets you buy. I mean, it's stuff we're used to. It wouldn't hurt your kidneys, would it?'

'Probably rot your liver,' suggested my father-in-law.

'Shouldn't think so,' Tiger defended his diet. 'Harmless . . . monosodium glutamate.'

'Wouldn't feed it to any dog of mine,' said the colonel.

'Right,' agreed Tiger. 'Wouldn't give it to our cats either. All right for Claire and me though.'

'It's doubtful,' I told him. 'There have been some articles against monosodium glutamate in the medical journals. Julia's banned foods with s.g. additive.'

'I say! Isn't that going a bit far? I mean, the ministry men passed monosodium glutamate for human consumption years ago, didn't they?'

'That doesn't make it any safer, now that we know more about the possible side-effects.'

'Something in that,' admitted Tiger. 'Still, I dare say the ministry men know what they're doing.'

'But you've just accused the ministry men of endangering our kidneys.'

'Absolutely. I'm telling you, Michael . . . this sheep-dip they're forcing on us is lethal. The use of it must be stopped.'

'You mean,' Julia gave Tiger an affectionate smile, 'you want my husband to stop it.'

'Of course. Who else?'

I picked up Tiger's bulging file. 'You hang on to this. I'm only doing a locum here, and in three weeks I'll be home in London. Better give these papers to Phil Brogan when he gets back.'

'By then it would be too late. We've all had the instructions from the Ag-Fish-Food Ministry. If I wait for Phil, half the Craftly farmers will have dipped their sheep in the damned poison.'

With young Mike still at the manor house, Julia and her father out – walking Biddy, and Mrs Cockman baking tarts in the kitchen, I had the patio and the big garden table to myself. I'd planned an afternoon game of golf. Instead, I got stuck into the papers Tiger had left with me. I surprised myself by becoming absorbed in the pros and cons of the ministry's preventive measures against sheep-scab.

I'd suspected Tiger of having developed one of his cranky eccentric theories – the kind I'd devastate in one well-considered and unanswerable sentence. but I soon had to change my mind. Despite all his zany ideas Tiger was no fool. Not only that; at all times, in all things, he had the passionate allegiance of his wife – including Claire's genius for charming people and her conviction that her husband was always right.

Perhaps he was. I recalled Tiger's most recent victory, not in the theatre but in real life. When the Arab sheik had bought Craftly Manor and taken to landing his helicopters on Tiger's land, the St George Clemens team of two had stopped all his motorized transport on their joint access drive very quietly and without going to the law. They'd done a thorough research job, discovered a binding traffic-clause in the seventeenth-century deeds of the land, and convinced Sheik Ahmed Habib that there was no way he could use the drive except for walking, riding on a horse or in horse-drawn vehicles.

According to the latest reports – relayed by the sheik's children and my son – sheik was currently flying around the

12

country, buying up a collection of carriages, including a French-built coach that had belonged to Mary, Queen of Scots.

Now, looking at the Ministry of Ag-Fish-Food's directives, it occurred to me that Tiger was all set to put the cat among the pigeons. Or rather – since he'd dropped the problem in my lap – it was a question of a *vet* among the pigeons.

The disease known as Psoroptic mange or sheep-scab *had* to be prevented or controlled. It was a nasty one that affected humans as well as animals. All the same, it seemed to me that Tiger did have a case against the remedy prescribed by the ministry.

Sheep-scab affects all parts of the body covered with wool, and the ears. Its life-cycle is thirteen to sixteen days, a rapid disease-progress. Being one of the worst sheep diseases it has to be notified – reported to the relevant authorities.

The mite which causes it feeds on the serum which oozes from the wounds made in the skin by the mite itself. the irritating poison produced by the mite makes the sheep scratch and rub themselves. This itching is usually the first symptom of the disease. The skin becomes thickened or even ulcerated, the wool falls out and the sick sheep become emaciated. The itching makes the animals rub themselves against fences so that the scabs of wounds fall off. This further spreads the disease and makes possible secondary infection of the wounds by bacteria.

The treatment consists of bathing affected animals in a dip, twice or even three times, at intervals of eight to twelve days. The chemicals used in the dip must be approved by the Ministry of Ag-Fish-Food. In 1938, dipping in Benzene Hexachloride or BHC was made compulsory; it was a method of preventing as well as treating sheep-scab. As a result of this stringently enforced measure the disease was eradicated in this country until 1952. Gradually dipping was abandoned. And then the disease re-appeared in 1973, and dipping became once again compulsory.

Tiger had included a copy of the order. It read: *To all Sheep Farmers. SHEEP-SCAB NATIONAL DIPPING AND MOVEMENT CONTROLS.*

As you will already know, it has been decided (in agreement with farmers' unions and other sheep farmers' representatives) that the sheep-scab situation is such that all sheep in England, Scotland and Wales must be dipped during the period 16 August to 13 November.

All sheep must be dipped during this period unless they are to be slaughtered during the period. Dipping must be carried out by immersion in a bath of single-dipping type sheep-dip approved by the Agriculture Departments for use against sheep-scab. Each sheep, including the head and ears must be immersed in the bath and kept immersed (except for the head and ears) for not less than 1 minute. Sheep-dips effective against sheep-scab contain the active ingredient gamma-BHC (benzene Hex-chaloride) and a certificate is included on the label saying that the dip has been approved for the purposes of the Sheep-Scab Orders . . .

The Sheep-Scab Orders require flock owners to notify the local authority of the date or dates on which they intend to dip their sheep within the prescribed period. The tear-off slip at the foot of the enclosed form J should be used for this purpose. This notice must be sent to the local authority in time to give them 3 clear days' notice of the dipping. A local authority Diseases of Animals Inspector or an officer of the ministry may attend the dipping . . .

A leaflet about dipping, safety and disposal of dips is enclosed . . .

In addition to the national dipping arrangements described above there will be special arrangements controlling the move-ment of sheep to markets during the period 1 July to 13 November. Markets in this context include also sales, fairs, exhibitions, and agricultural and fatstock shows . . .

All sheep sent to market etc. (other than sheep intended for immediate slaughter) during this period must have been dipped during the 56 days preceding the market and since they were

14

dipped they must have been kept separate from undipped sheep. The sheep must be accompanied to market by the owner's declaration of dipping, a copy of which is enclosed (SSD 1). This declaration must be surrendered to the Diseases of Animals Inspector at the market . . .

Sheep which are to be sent to market for sale for immediate slaughter need not be dipped but must be accompanied to market by a licence. This licence may be obtained from the local authority (at the given address). The enclosed form of declaration that the sheep are intended for sale for immediate slaughter (SSUD2) should be completed when applying to the local authority for a licence . . .

You should continue to be on the look out for scab in your flock and be particularly careful to examine sheep you buy. You must notify the police or the Divisional Veterinary Officer of any disease or slightest suspicion of disease . . .

With these instructions there was a great deal of sensible advice on the most effective type of dipping baths, on the siting of baths, pens and forcing pens, and sorting gates. The ministry had even included a note on the psychology of sheep: *Will follow one another. Prefer to move uphill, prefer to move towards open country i.e to freedom. Will move away from buildings. Flow better around slight corners and curves. Are easily frightened. Move towards other sheep.*

I was beginning to wonder what the fuss was about when I came upon some pages marked with the skull and cross-bones symbol for *poison*. The first of them was a Ministry of Ag-Fish-Food leaflet which pointed out that gamma-BHC dip may be dangerous to humans, animals fish and stream life. It was therefore illegal to allow the dip to enter a waterway, a public sewer, fields under drainage systems, boreholes, wells, springs or ponds. That certainly made its safe disposal rather difficult.

Even more specifically, the leaflet admitted that certain ingredients in dips may be temporarily absorbed into the sheep's system thus presenting a health-risk to man if the sheep has been slaughtered too soon after dipping. Some constituents of dip solution can also be absorbed through the human skin and the ministry was advising users that they were required by law to wear specified protective clothing when opening the container, or diluting, mixing or transferring the dip from one container to another.

Tiger had certainly done his homework. He had obtained reports on gamma Benzene Hexachloride from the poisons' unit of a London teaching hospital and from the Royal Society. Neither was encouraging about the use of this chemical. Plants were known to absorb it, thus becoming toxic to the insects feeding on them. Some sheep with long coats had been found to be unfit for human consumption though the other dipped sheep of the flock had been safe. Stored grain had been found to absorb gamma Benzene Hexachloride in the vapour stage.

The medical report was definitely worrying. Apparently acute poisoning from the gamma isomer could lead to tremors and convulsions in humans. Chronic poisoning results in an increase in the size of the liver and permanent deposits of the poison in blood, spleen, muscle, brain, adrenals and kidney. What this meant was that the poison was cumulative and once having entered the body remained and built up. According to the reports Tiger had gathered, gamma Benzene Hexachloride was a poisonous substance that did not get weaker and less harmful in time, neither in a living body not in plants, soil or water. Continuous use of BHC was liable to pollute the countryside, our food and finally our bodies.

I was still prepared not to condemn BHC, telling myself that the ministry must have considered its dangers before prescribing it as *the* sheep-dip for the whole country. And yet large public organizations were cumbersome and learned slowly. It wouldn't be the first time that our administrators had passed a dangerous substance for general use until some fanatic, like a single-minded scientist or someone like Tiger, put a stop to it.

What finally persuaded me to keep a very open mind on the subject was Tiger's correspondence with the relevant authorities. He'd asked time and again whether there wasn't

16

a sheep-dip that did *not* contain BHC; and time and again his question had been ignored or evaded.

A second reading of those papers convinced me that Tiger was not being unreasonable. Animals certainly had to be protected from sheep-scab, but I couldn't believe that the gamma BHC dip was the only one that could serve the purpose. Nor did the fact that the ministry literature did not mention an alternative dip mean that such a dip didn't exist.

In bed, late at night, I talked to Julia about it.

'We're not staying in Craftly very long,' she said diplomatically.

'I know.'

'So what can you do about it?'

'See one or two people.'

She laughed. 'That's what I like about you, Michael . . . you're so informative.'

'Well, I have no plans.'

'As yet. But look out; this sheep-dip thing smells of trouble.'

CHAPTER 3

Mrs Cockman gave us an early breakfast because Julia had to take Mike back to school. We knew from experience the reason for Mike's unusual silence. He'd had a happy weekend with his Arab friends and the multi-ethnic beetle project, but now he was looking forward to telling his school chums, and – above all – his brother Andy, his adventures. He was already rehearsing the stories in his mind, turning the most trivial incident into high drama. The temporary disappearance of his grandfather's bitch would become a tale of the whole village searching for Biddy. And as I had been rash enough to talk about the sheep-dip in front of him, he was quite likely to tell Andy – swearing him to secrecy, of course – that the poisoned people of Craftly would develop pointed ears like the space-travellers in *Startrek*.

As Julia and Mike got into the car, my father-in-law announced that he'd stay another day or two. Bachelor had come to visit Biddy and the two of them were playing on the lawn like a couple of pups. the colonel said it would be unfair to separate them just yet.

At ten to nine Josephine, the receptionist, arrived and we went across to the surgery. Josephine was a tall, weather-beaten woman around thirty and the most attractive thing about her was her deep, soft voice – the kind of voice animals would find soothing.

'After morning surgery,' she told me, 'you might have time to visit Miss Shrapnell's kennels. Some pups there due for inoculation or boosters.' She opened the door to the waiting room, took in the scene, and closed it again. 'You shouldn't have any operating to do; not this morning. But I'll be handy if you want me . . . There's the odd owner who can't bear holding her pet while you examine it.'

18

First to enter the surgery was Tail with a little mongrel which had some characteristics of a smooth-haired terrier. Tail, so called because she'd been the tail-end of a large farming family, had been one of the first people I'd met in Craftly – more than ten years ago. She'd been a schoolgirl then – quick, clever and stage-struck. She was now secretary to the vice-chancellor of Outpost College and the manager of the Craftly Drama Society. It was her doing that the society had achieved its own little theatre and was performng ambitious classical or prestige modern plays such as Tiger's *Psht*.

'Hello Uncle Michael,' she greeted me.

'You're too old now to call me uncle.'

She laughed. 'Michael isn't respectful enough.' She lifted the dog and put it on the examination table. 'This is Patch.'

Obviously. He had a black patch around one eye, black socks and a black tail. The rest of him was white. The most attractive thing about him were the ears, large, softly feathered ears which stood up alertly. The little mongrel, so friendly that the tail was wagging the dog, appeared to have inherited the boisterous energy of terrier plus beagle.

'What's the matter with him?' I asked Tail.

'Nothing, I hope. He's had his injections . . . the RSPCA have seen to it. And I've wormed him. It's just . . . I want you to look him over. I must be sure he's okay.'

'Patch isn't your kind of animal.' I was puzzled. Tail, living with her sister and brother-in-law, had never gone in for pet dogs. There were enough animals on the Thorntons' farm.

'He isn't mine,' said Tail. 'Peter and I got him for the children.'

'Peter?'

'Peter Ford. He's the new teacher at the village school. Jenny . . . that's his young sister . . . lives with him. The other sister, Ruth, was married to a businessman in Belfast. He's been killed in a bomb attack. Ruth was injured and she's still in hospital. Peter and Jenny are looking after her kids. Jill's six, Tony's nine. We thought the children should

have something . . . well . . .' For once Tail was at a loss
for words. 'You see, they were with their parents . . .'

'When the bomb went off?'

She nodded. 'Perhaps Patch will . . . make a difference.'

As I stroked the dog his whole body wriggled with
pleasure. Clearly, he was going to be a very unhygienic pet,
the kind that would take flying leaps onto the owner's bed
or even insist on sharing the pillow. 'All right, Patch, calm
down. Let's take a look at you.'

He was a sturdy little animal, about nine months old and
in excellent condition. Not a stray, explained Tail, but born
at the RSPCA kennels. They'd found a good home for his
mother at Nether Craftly.

'He's fine,' I assured Tail.

She lifted him down and put on his lead. 'Thanks. I'll
take him to Peter's so the kids will have him when they get
back from school . . . Uncle Michael, I want you to meet
Peter.'

Her sudden shyness, so out of character, took me by
surprise. 'Bring him along.'

'When?'

'Any evening. You don't need a formal invitation, do
you?'

'No.' She gave the familar urchin grin. 'Love to Aunt
Julia. Bye.'

So it had happened at last. Tail, a young woman in love. I
watched her through the window, running to her Mini with
Patch prancing at her heels.

Josephine's assessment of the morning surgery turned out
to be right. Nothing complicated. An old lady, whose
canary needed to have its claws trimmed; a child whose cat
had a mild eye-infection; a boisterous labrador which had
tried to bash through a hole in a fence and cut his shoulder.
There was time to visit Craftly Kennels before lunch and I
went off in the practice's Japanese hatch-back.

Beyond the compact village centre I followed a leafy,
winding road through pastures and fields, along a dew-pond
and a common overgrown with gorse and brambles. A

thicket of elderberries half concealed the kennel's hanging shield, but I assumed that the nose and front-paws of a dog indicated the right address.

I stopped the car, opened the wired gate and drove on along a drive of deep potholes to a Nissen hut marked *office*.

'*Mon dieu!* You left the gate open!' accused a voice with a strong French accent – a throaty nightclub voice.

'I did not.' I switched off the engine and got out.

'Owners always leave the gate open.'

'I'm not a pet owner.' There was no one in sight. 'I'm the vet.'

The rhododendron bushes beside the hut parted and a strapping woman in fringed suede trousers, a see-through black shirt and a wide-brimmed bush-hat confronted me. She was about forty and would have been quite handsome if she hadn't looked so aggressive.

'Mr Brogan's my vet.' She took stock of me.

'He's on holiday. I'm Michael Morton, his locum.'

She became a little less belligerent. 'One just can't rely on *anybody*. But my puppies need their shots, so what the hell?'

The boarding kennels and a well-equipped operating room and *nursing home* for dogs were immaculately clean and comfortable. Mrs Shrapnell's own dogs, spaniels, were good looking, well-bred animals.

She stood over me while I inoculated her six puppies and then led me to her bungalow. It stood in the middle of a rough field which was alive with rabbits.

'Damned farmers shoot them,' she explained. 'They're not fools . . . they know they're safe here.'

'If you don't mind them . . .'

She laughed. 'I've given up growing vegetables.'

'Don't the dogs chase them?'

'Not my dogs. The bunnies are so tame, they play with my spaniels, If animals grow up together they don't hurt each other.' She opened her back door. 'There. Look at this.'

This was a big goose, reclining on straw under the kitchen

21

sink, beside a sleeping cat. In a basket by the Aga cooker an old cocker spaniel wagged his tail and made a brave effort to rise and greet his owner.

'What do you think of him, Mr Morton?'

The hindlegs of the dog stumbled like a spastic's, the back was humped. 'Slipped disk. Are his bladder and bowels working?'

'Perfectly . . . I expect you want to pump poor old Tommy full of nandrolone.' It was a statement, a rather belligerent one.

'I don't want to touch him, Mrs Shrapnell.'

'Don't know what to do, eh? She sounded very French again.

'I know when to do nothing. Tommy's not in pain, and he's recovering perfectly well without treatment.'

'No treatment you say! I'm giving him physiotherapy. My husband . . . he left me, the dirty pig, for a French au pair girl . . . Mr Astley Shrapnell flattered himself that he was the only one who could look after dogs. He thought the kennels would go bankrupt without him. Well?' she glared at me. 'What's wrong with my kennels?'

'Nothing. They're first rate.'

'There! Have a beer.'

'Thanks.' Oddly enough I was glad I had the time. When Madame Shrapnell smiled she was quite fascinating.

'My spaniel pups are good, eh?' She took a couple of lagers from the fridge and poured them into heavy glass tumblers. 'I'll get a hundred and twenty each, eh?

'They're worth it.'

'Well . . .selling my animals to the highest bidder is a little like the slave trade. But I must pay the rates and the electricity bills. My ex-husband . . the pig . . . took all the money out of the joint account. After twenty years of marriage!'

'Shame,' I muttered.

'He's an idiot. the only time I miss him is when I want to go out for an evening. The boy who helps me can't always come, and I hate leaving the animals. Tonight I'll worry all the time, but I can't miss another rehearsal. We're doing Viscount St George Clemens's new play.'

'*Psht*?'

'Ah, you know Tiger! He's a genius. *Psht* might have been written for me.'

'I thought it was a play without words.'

'Of course. that's what makes it so perfect. No problems with my accent. All I have to do is take a man by the collar and tear his shirt . . . It's a wonderful, wonderful sound . . . the only sound in the whole play. The audience will be – what's the word I want – Oh yes, the drama will electrocute the audience.'

I managed to keep a straight face. 'I'll be seeing the play, I expect. Must be on my way . . .'

Madame Shrapnell followed me out. 'Visit us again Mr Morton. I want to be sure that Tommy's back is making good progress.'

'No need to waste your money.' I almost fell over a rabbit.

She was quick. 'A social visit, I mean . . . There are things you should know about Craftly. Do you know that we're being poisoned?'

'I've heard . . . rumours.'

'About the sheep-dip, eh? It's criminal! Faceless ministry men making the farmers pollute the soil . . . creating a danger to life! Look at my rabbits. Can't you see it? my whole paddock strewn with these silky little bodies . . .' Haunting tragedy darkened Madame Shrapnell's big eyes. 'Dead! all dead. How can England slaughter the innocents? France, yes. But England! You know Mr Morton, this attack on my bunnies proves it; England's going to the dogs.' Her gumbooted foot pushed aside an inquisitive rabbit – none too gently. 'You're married? Yes, I can tell. Married men . . . they have this cat-at-the-milk look. Never mind, do come again. And this time, shut the gate.'

Josephine's note read, *please call at Chalk Farm, Bill Bowles, query mastitis.* Making it my last visit of the day, because there was no telling how much time it would take, I took the long way round the perimeter of the farm. The cowsheds and barns were old but well repaired and the animals – a dairy herd of Jerseys – looked sleek and healthy. I reckoned that Mr Bowles was not the modern, scientific kind of farmer but certainly an experienced one.

I found him in the stable yard at the side of the house, a short, rugged man in his sixties. He was watching a young girl groom a pony.

I introduced myself and he responded with a nod. 'My daughter, Bobby,' he said, smiling at the girl. 'She does my books, when she isn't too busy training Badger . . . or grooming him.'

'It's our Bluebell father wants you to see.' Bobby was stroking Badger's nose.

'Your idea, not mine. Let's get it over with.' Bowles turned and made for the cowsheds at the bottom of the hill.

'You have an autumn calving herd?' I asked.

'That's right.' He led me into the smallest shed. There was only one cow in the stalls. 'I've isolated Bluebell. You tell me what's wrong with her.'

'You think she's got mastitis?'

'Not me. But I want you to examine her.'

Bluebell's temperature was normal and so was her pulse. She was standing quietly, not paddling with her feet, and she remained unperturbed while I examined her udders. Each quarter produced milk which was entirely free from blood, pus or flocculence.

'Well?' asked Bowles.

'I can find not sign of mastitis. What's made you suspect it? A lower yield?

'No. You're sure Bluebell's sound?'

'One can't be one hundred per cent sure without laboratory tests . . . a cell count.'

'Right. Get the tests done, Mr Morton.'

'I'd say it's a waste of money in this case . . . unless you have good reasons for suspecting mastitis in this cow.'

'There's no good reason,' said Farmer Bowles angrily.

'But I want it in writing that Bluebell's all right.'

'As you wish.' I picked up my bag and we left the cow, munching serenely.

Back in the yard, Bobby had stabled her pony and was feeding it an apple. 'How's Bluebell?'

'Fit,' her father told her. 'But I'm having tests done . . . just to keep you quiet.'

'Have you told Mr Morton what it's all about?'

'What for?'

'Oh father! You're hopeless.'

'Very well then.' Bowles looked sheepish. 'It's like this, Mr Morton . . . Some time ago we had the diseases of animals inspector here – young fool, name of Short. They had mastitis over at Nether Craftly. He tested my animals and said Bluebell was sick . . . told me to get rid of her. My best cow!'

'So, you didn't.'

'Shorty doesn't know what he's talking about . . . half the time. When you're dealing with animals you can't go by computers or the book all the time . . . as any farmer knows.'

Bobby had joined us at my car and was standing with a hand on her father's shoulder. I had the impression that the small, wiry girl – Bowles' only child – was trying to be a son as well as a daughter. 'Dad isolated Bluebell,' she explained, 'and gave her a calf to feed.'

'She'd lost her own?'

'Right.' Bowles gave me a friendly grin. 'Bluebell was upset, that's what it was. When Shorty tested the milk . . . usual way, with the cup covered with gauze . . . he found some solid white threads. But it wasn't what he said. *I* knew it wasn't mastitis. The calf soon got the milk clear.'

'And now you want lab confirmation that you were right.'

'I do, Mr Morton. Shorty will be back, asking questions, and I'm going to have the answers. That boy will have to learn a thing or two before he starts throwing his weight about.'

25

'I bet he'll turn up to watch us dip the sheep,' said Bobby.

'That's all right. He won't lay down the law . . . not after what happened with Bluebell. I reckon he isn't all that stupid.'

I asked, 'What sheep dip will you be using?'

'The ministry's recommended BHC – as usual.' Bowles' bright blue eyes looked thoughtful. 'Tiger been at you, has he?'   'Well, he isn't keen on BHC. What's your opinion?'

'I think he's right.'

'But you'll stick to BHC just the same.'

'No option. If Tiger had come to us in the summer . . . telling us about an alternative dip which is accepted by the ministry . . . we'd be using it.'

'He's been trying to find such an alternative, for months.'

'I reckon he didn't get any change out of Dick Craven.'

'Who's he?'

'Ministry vet.'

I remembered the signature on a letter in Tiger's file, a typical bland administrator's letter which effectively avoided the question of alternatives to the BHC dip.

'Trouble is,' said Bobby, 'that we've got to dip our sheep before the middle of November. It's the law.'

'So you've got three weeks.'   'I know,' agreed Bowles. 'But that doesn't give us much time. Dipping's a big job. There's all the preparations and finding extra hands. Don't get me wrong Mr Morton, I agree with Tiger. If there's a less poisonous dip than BHC the ministry should let us know. If Tiger comes up with an answer for next year we'll be glad to stop using BHC. You can tell his livestock manager.'

'I will.' I put my case in the car. 'I'll send you the results of the lab tests.'

I decided to pass on Farmer Bowles' message on my way home. Anyway it was a good excuse for renewing the old friendship with Willard, Duke of Alanspring, and his man

26

Masters. I remembered with nostalgia the elegant Mayfair house, where the greyhound, Grey Rainbow, had become one of my first patients, the damp country cottage, where they'd moved when the duke hadn't been able to afford his London life any longer, and the luxurious American period when the duke had been married to the widow of millionaire Miller-Hundling. By what Tiger had told me the marriage had not improved the duke's finances.

At the flint wall of Craftly Manor I slowed down. The new Arab owners must have managed to get building permission for extensive alterations, a dozen bathrooms and all, because the great house was cocooned in a web of scaffolding. Beyond it I caught a glimpse of something large and white. At first I thought it was the kind of temporary accommodation that builders put up for themselves so as to satisfy the workmen's demands for comfortable hourly teabreaks, but a couple of hundred yards on the building turned out to be Tiger's house – that curious round structure on stilts which looked like a flying saucer. Strangely enough the white saucer did not look bizarre in its country setting; the great oak trees were taking care of that.

I turned into Tiger's drive, skirted the saucer, and stopped at the Manor Cottage at the end of the lane. A dozen sheep were grazing in the adjoining field and a couple of children were climbing the stile of the public footpath on the south side.

Suddenly a small black and white dog came leaping out of a ditch and went racing at the sheep, barking furiously. The sheep veered, jostling one another, and stampeded towards the vegetable garden.

The door of the cottage was flung open and there stood Masters with a gun in his hands. Too angry to notice me, he raised it, muzzle following the movements of the dog.

'Masters, if ever I see you raise a gun to a dog again I'll dispense with your services.' The duke looked as put out as I'd ever seen him. The handsome face under the white hair was still looking flushed.

27

'Yes, your Grace,' answered Masters, stolidly.

'Country life's turning you into a savage.'

'No, your Grace.'

'No? What d'you mean?'

'If I may say so, I'm country born and bred. We can't have dogs chase our sheep, your Grace. It's bad for them. They might have hurt themselves.'

'Very well, Masters. But *dogs first* in future . . . Come in Michael.' The duke put a hand on my arm. 'Have a drink. Our elderberry wine's first rate.'

The little glass porch was as full of flowering plants as a greenhouse. An ornately carved chair covered in blue velvet suggested that it was the duke's favourite spot. With the charm that was his greatest survival asset, he offered me the *throne* and sat down on the small wooden bench. Masters emerged from the dark interior of the cottage with crystal glasses on a silver tray.

'Down the hatch.' The duke took a swig. 'Well, what d'you think of our Manor Cottage wine?'

'Tastes good,' I said, and meant it.

'Damn sight better than the hootch one buys in André's. Their stuff's full of chemicals these days . . . Good to see you, Michael. What are you doing down here? How's the family?'

While I answered the duke's questions and gave him the message from Farmer Bowles, I kept an eye on the footpath. The children had captured their dog . . . it was Patch, of course . . . and were wandering towards the cottage.

'Farmers,' snorted the Duke. 'They're all the same . . . quite willing to support Tiger in principle. But none of them have helped Tiger in finding an alternative to the BHC dip . . . And none of them, as far as we know, has taken the matter up with the ministry . . . How d'you like my girls?' A couple of goats had come squeezing into the porch. They had unusual cream and brown markings and alert faces which somehow reminded me of the devil in one of Mike's story books. They crowded in on the duke, their rears knocking over some flowerpots. 'What do you think of them Michael?'

'Unusual.'

'Certainly are. The strain comes from Samarkand. Going to breed these beauties. Give it a few years and my goats will be as popular as . . . as . . . er, other pedigree pets. Productive pets at that. Milk, you know.'

'Do you like goats' milk?'

'Can't stand it as a matter of fact. But if one puts this thing on a sound business footing . . .'

Grey Rainbow, the greyhound who'd been allergic to hares, had been a business venture . . . the most engaging and abortive I'd ever known. One had to admire the duke for persisting in the most unlikely schemes for making his fortune. Yet, there was no accounting for fashion in pets.

The children had almost reached the cottage. 'I'd better have a word with them.' I told the duke that Tony and Jill had lost their father in Belfast and that their mother was still in hospital. 'Tail got them the pup.'

'Take their minds off the troubles over there.'

'Yes, but Patch will be trouble if they don't keep him off farm animals.' I went out to the gate and whistled.

Patch pricked up his feathery ears and pulled the little girl up to me. Whether he remembered me or not, he was wriggling with pleasure.

'Come on Patch,' pleaded Jill.

Tony took the lead from her. 'You mustn't pull him.'

'He's pulling me.'

I said, 'You'll have to train him . . . First of all, don't ever let him loose in the fields. Farm animals are frightened of strange dogs. Always keep Patch on the lead.'

'Was the man going to shoot him dead?' asked Tony.

'No.' Luckily Jill answered the awkward question. 'They don't do that here. He just wanted to stop Patch chasing the sheep.'

'But he had a gun . . . and guns are for shooting people,' insisted Tony.

How could I refute such logic? Knowledge acquired at first hand in the endless, miserable Ulster civil war. I said,

'The gun you've seen is different. It's the kind farmers have for shooting . . . well . . . foxes who steal their chickens.'

Tony and Jill looked at one another. 'You know the bangs we heard,' said Jill 'Tail told us it was just people shooting at bits of paper.'

Why hadn't I thought of that?

'Targets,' Tony nodded. 'They don't shoot foxes in Craftly either,' he informed me. 'They go around with foxes on the lead . . . like us and Patch.'

'They do?' Thinking of my own son, I assumed that Tony's imagination was equally vivid.

'S'right,' Jill assured me. 'Custer's a fox, see. And Custer eats Pedigree Chum so he's always going shopping in the High Street.'

'Master, did you hear that?' There was a note of triumph in the duke's voice. 'If you can't tell the difference between a corgi and a fox you should stick to sheep.'

'I do, your Grace,' said Masters, 'I do.'

'What did you say the name of that fox is?' the Duke asked the children.

'Custer.'

'Well, it's not what I'd call *my* fox. Masters, we'll have to think about that.'

'I hope your Grace isn't thinking of acquiring a fox.'

'One should always be prepared.'

'Sir, your goats wouln't like it.'

'There you may have a point, Masters.'

CHAPTER 4

Morning surgery had been so quiet and uneventful that Josephine suggested my visiting at least one patient before lunch. 'Hugo Lavinski would fit in nicely.'

'Hugo who?' I asked.

Josephine consulted her message book. 'It sounded like Lavinski, but my spelling's probably wrong. Anyway . . . he's in digs at 55 High Street. Wants you to see his fox.'

'Is that the one that goes out on a lead?'

'That's right.'

'Did he say what's the matter with the animal?'

'No . . . just that it's more troublesome than usual.'

'Doesn't sound like a fond pet-owner.'

'I don't think Hugo is.'

'Why keep a fox then?'

Josephine laughed. 'That's what the whole village wants to know.'

I went along the patio into the house, vaguely thinking that Julia might like to visit the fox with me and give me a hand. No doubt; Julia's better than I at handling unusual or wild animals.

Mrs Cockman, plump and rosy, was cooking something that smelled good. 'Mrs Morton and her dad have taken the dog for a walk,' she told me. 'She's funny, Biddy is; she sounds like she's talking when she wants out . . . and the colonel gives in every time. Such a gentleman, the colonel.'

I left the hatch-back and our own TR2 in the yard, baking in the sun, and walked down the lane to the village. I had a good idea why Julia and her father had taken the colonel's car; Biddy preferred riding to walking when she wasn't racing along in parks or open country. Julia maintained that the colonel had always been a better father to his alsatian bitches than to her.

31

I turned the corner at the church, passed the Craftly Arms and began to look for number 55, watched by Simpkins of the hardware shop and Miss Phoebe Langor.

'Morning Mr Morton. Anything I can do for you?'

'Know where I can find the fox?'

'Above the newsagent's. That's where the Polish gentleman's in digs.'

'I don't think he's Polish,' said Miss Phoebe. 'He speaks with a Cockney accent.'

'You're right there ma'am,' agreed Simpkins. 'Born in London, he told our Prudence, but his dad came from Poland. Something funny about him though.'

'Clearly.' Miss Phoebe squared her shoulders. 'Man who keeps a fox must be round the twist.'

'It's his job like, ma'am. That's what our Prudence says.'

'Rubbish, Mr Simpkins. the man's been spinning a tale. A job indeed!'

'It could be something scientific like.'

'It could be, if the man were studying a pig. Next to humans, pigs are the most intelligent of the mammals. Isn't that right Mr Morton?'

'I'm no expert,' I said vaguely.

'I am,' snapped Miss Phoebe, 'as a member of the executive of the Royal Pig Society . . . and a not entirely unknown painter of pigs.'

I edged away, almost colliding with one of those shopping baskets on wheels. 'Well . . . thanks for your help.'

Number 55 was on a narrow door beside a rack of beat-up paperbacks. As I opened it I heard a thunder of running footsteps, followed by a splash of water.

'If you're the vet,' shouted a breathless voice, 'we're in the bathroom.'

It was a weird sight; the short young man with black, curly hair, dressed in khaki shorts and thick rubber gloves, struggling to keep a red fox in the bath-tub. The fox was wearing a leather muzzle. It was leaping furiously at the high sides of the tub, making the water slosh out in all directions.

'Sorry we're not decent,' apologized Hugo Lavinski. 'I meant to have the brute all ready for you . . . presentable.' The eyes behind the thick spectacles were laughing. 'But the bastard had other ideas.'

'Perhaps he doesn't like water,' I said.

'Ever tried *not* bathing a fox? Well . . . the stink's got to be smelled to be believed.' Holding the fox by the scruff he began to rinse off the soap suds. 'Steady, Custer.'

Custer wasn't exactly steady, but the scrabbling and spashing became less violent. Perhaps experience had taught him that the shower was the last part of the operation. When Hugo finally manhandled the fox out of the bath I noticed that the left hind paw looked sore.

'Yes,' said Hugo. 'It's the paw. Mind if we stay in the bathroom? easier to catch him here.'

'All right. I suppose the sore's a self-inflicted injury.'

'Yes, he's been biting it.'

'Foxes aren't meant to live in digs in Craftly High Street.'

'Couldn't agree with you more.'

'Then why . . .'

Hugo sighed. 'Okay, I'll tell you all about Custer. By the way, it's me who's given him the name . . . You know, *Custer's last stand,* because he always puts up a good fight against soap and water. And don't tell me bathing him's cruel. Me having to live with the stinker's much tougher.'

'Who's forcing you?'

'It's my job. I'm a copper.'

'A policeman!'

'Don't mention it in the village, will you. They wouldn't believe it. All the same . . . I'm in the police scientific development branch. My chief's got to dream up new ideas of crime detection. His thing's finding bodies . . . you know, people who've been nurdered and buried nice and tidy.'

'Aren't you using dogs for that kind of thing?'

'Yes. But training dogs and paying the handlers is expensive. So the big chief thought he'd get animals on the

33

cheap maybe. He reckoned vultures would be the job.
Trouble is, the vultures we imported didn't like the English
climate. So he came up with foxes. He figures that foxes
wouldn't have to be trained because it's natural for them to
dig up dead things. Well . . . he hasn't lived with Custer;
that's all I can say.'

'Custer's got the wrong instincts?'

'Oh no, he's got the right instincts. No matter were I take
him *he'll* find a vixen.'

'What's the point of continuing your experiment?'

'Custer and me will be allowed to go our separate ways;
you bet. But not until we've sweated out the allotted time
and the big cheese is satisfied that any sensible fox is more
interested in . . . lady foxes than murdered ladies.'

'All right. Can you hold Custer while I look at his paw?'

Hugo pulled on his gloves again and made a successful
dive for the fox. The paw was not too bad, but it was
obvious that Custer had been busy chewing off the scabs of
earlier bites.

'We've got to put something on the paw . . . something
he doesn't like the taste of. I once knew a fox who bit his
tail; what put him off was tonic water.'

'Doesn't work with Custer.'

'How do you know?'

'I've tried it. Read all about it in your book.'

'Difficult to know what to suggest. A tranquilliser should
be the last resort. The fox should just be in a more congenial
environment.'

Hugo grinned, 'So should I, Mr Morton. What you're
really saying is . . . we should put something that tastes
'orrible on Custer's paw.'

'Something non-poisonous.'

'I'm a copper, not a murderer . . . whatever I feel about
foxes.' Hugo let go of the squirming animal and Custer
streaked under the linen cupboard. 'Any stuff I put on his
paw will be hit or miss, won't it?'

'Just about.'

'That's great! The big cheese didn't say about *nursing* the

34

brute.'

'I'll make up a prescription. You can pick it up later.'

Hugo, who'd been looking at the tubes and bottles on the bathroom shelf, picked up an aerosol capped with a pink, plastic nude. 'There's this,' he muttered.

'What is it?'

'After-shave.' He plucked off the nude and squirted the stuff at the ceiling. The pungent smell – not unlike tom cat – made both of us cough. 'Girlfriend gave it to me,' spluttered Hugo. 'Ex-girlfriend now.'

'I'm not surprised.'

'Bet Custer wouldn't like this on his paw.'

'I wouldn't inflict it on my worst enemy.'

'Okay, I don't hate Custer that much. I'll settle for the prescription.' Hugo opened the bathroom door for me, a nimble shove preventing Custer from escaping.

The fox's throaty growl followed me all the way down the stairs. I felt thankful that I wouldn't be present when Custer was trying to lick asafoetida off his paw.

The High Street smelled worse than any London main road; the diesel fumes, emitted from lorries and juggernauts, made me feel choked. I was reflecting on the damage the heavy traffic would do to the beautiful Tudor and Queen Anne houses when I saw a swirl of spaniel tails. It was moving towards me, bunched together around the booted legs of Madame Shrapnell. The cavalcade of dogs was being overtaken by Bobby Bowles on her pony, Badger, and on the other side of the street Tail and a bearded young man were coming out of the school yard.

What happened next was so sudden that it stopped the lot of us dead in our tracks. A builders' van, driven by a long-haired cowboy, came shooting through the street much too fast. A car going in the opposite direction almost collided with it and the screaming of its brakes made the pony shy onto the pavement. As Bobby tried to control Badger he reared on his hind legs, sent her flying over a fence and went down in the middle of the road.

'Mon dieu!' Mrs Shrapnell let go her dog-leads and made

for the pony. 'He's broken a leg! Don't stand there like imbeciles! Help me! The poor horse!' She made a dive and grabbed me by the sleeve. 'You're a vet . . . this is your *affaire* . . .'

'I'd better see to Bobby.'

'The girl's all right.' She held on to me. 'His leg! Is it broken?'

Tail and the bearded man had entered the yard of the Craftly Arms and helped Bobby off the yew hedge. She seemed shaken but in one piece. A man who'd come out of the pub was holding up the traffic. The moment Badger saw his rider he scrabbled with his front-hooves, heaved and picked himself up. Bobby, stroking his neck, quietly led him to the edge of the road.

'If you don't know how to control your horse,' attacked Mrs Shrapnell, 'you shouldn't be riding in the High Street.'

'And you shouldn't let your dogs roam all over the road.' snapped Bobby.

Mrs Shrapnell made off fast. 'Get the vet to examine your horse,' she called over her shoulder, 'or I'll report you to the RSPCA.'

'That's enough,' said Tail, with unexpected authority. She caught two of the spaniels and gave the leads to Mrs Shrapnell. 'If you want to stay in Tiger's play you've got to change your thinking. How could you play a woman who cares for all humanity and . . . and feel more for the horse than for Bobby? You've got to develop the right vibes, Mrs Shrapnell.'

'Yes, Tail,' Shrapnell apologized meekly.

Tail turned to Bobby. 'If you like I'll ride him home for you.'

'No, thanks. I'm all right.'

'Sure you haven't broken your collar bone?' asked the bearded man.

Bobby laughed. 'If I have, it wouldn't be the first time . . . Really. I'm all right.'

'Uncle Michael, how about Badger?' Tail watched me complete a quick examination of the pasterns.

36

'There doesn't seem to be any damage.'

'Oh . . .' Tail took the bearded man's hand. 'This is Peter, Uncle Michael.'

He smiled. 'You've been country-training my nephew and niece. Masters complained about Patch chasing sheep, but – thanks to you – he thinks it won't happen again.'

'I don't think it will. They're sensible kids, Tony and Jill.'

'Hope you're right.' There was a shadow of concern in Peter's eyes. 'I'd be happier if they weren't so quiet . . . especially about Belfast.'

Bobby had mounted her pony. 'Thanks everybody. See you.'

We watched her walk Badger down the street. Neither seemed the worse for the fall.

The man from the pub joined us. 'Bit of luck she was thrown on the only hedge in the High Street . . . Join me for a drink?'

'No thanks, Mr Craven,' Tail refused. 'My sister's expecting us for lunch.'

'How about you, Morton?'

It suddenly came to me; he was Dick Craven, the divisional veterinary officer, and I'd had dealings with him years ago – though I couldn't remember what dealings. I accepted his invitation. I had a vague idea that he might answer a few question.

Dick Craven was what Julia calls *ish,* thinnish, fairish, with bluish eyes and fortyish. As we were propping up the Craftly Arms bar I had the impression that something was missing; and then it came to me . . . the bowler hat. Dick Craven, the prototype of a civil servant, really did look incomplete without a bowler hat.

'What are you doing down here?' he asked me. 'Thought you were in practice in London.'

'I am . . . Just doing a locum for Phil Brogan.'

'That's what happened last time,' he said, enigmatically. Not quite the same thing – London pussies and Craftly cows, are they?'

'Not quite.' He'd given me the ideal opening. 'As a matter of fact I'd appreciate your advice.'

'Oh yes?'

'This business of sheep-dipping.'

'It's compulsory.'

'I know. I've had one or two queries about the dip.'

'Oh yes?' This time his question sounded more cautious.

'Your ministry's ordered the farmers to use Benzene Hexachloride . . .'

'Well . . . er . . . we've *recommended* BHC.'

'So there are alternative dips approved by you?'

He finished his beer. 'No one's denying that there are other dips which are effective against sheep-scab.'

'Recommended by you?'

'Any farmer can use a dip of his choice, provided we approve the formula.'

'Good, then your office would be able to supply me with a list of alternative approved dips?'

'Afraid not.' Dick Craven looked past me into the middle distance.

'If BHC isn't the only dip farmers are permitted to use, you must have *something* . . . a list or a note or a memo . . . something that tells farmers what alternative dips you'd accept.'

'Nothing like that at my offices.'

'So where would a local farmer get the information?'

'Oh . . . er . . .' Dick Craven yawned. 'He could try Mr Short, the diseases of animals inspector.'

'One farmer did, and Mr Short referred him to your office.'

'Did he write a letter to us?'

'Several letters.'

'I expect one of my girls answered them.'

'Yes . . . sending the same damned silly answer every time; that the sheep must be dipped by 13th November and that dips effective against sheep-scab contain the active ingredient gamma BHC.'

Craven frowned. 'That's perfectly correct.'

I couldn't tell whether he was stupid or playing a game. 'Look the answers from your office may be correct but they just don't answer the question, do they? I know at least two farmers who'd prefer a less poisonous sheep-dip. They don't like the idea of permanent soil pollution. Surely it's up to your office to give them the information they want.'

'Look here, Morton . . . the great majority of farmers are perfectly happy with BHC. If I were you I wouldn't worry about the odd crank.'

'You are the ministry vet. You are paid by the public to do a job . . . and you're not doing your job if you ignore *cranks,* who are also members of the salary-paying public.'

'I say, Morton! That's a little uncalled for, isn't it?'

'A timely reminder, that's all. I wouldn't insult you by suggesting that you have shares in the firm that manufactures BHC.'

I'm glad to hear that,' he picked up his briefcase, ready for flight.

'Pity we'll have to waste time going to your minister for the information.'

'Take my advice, Morton. Don't waste too much time . . . because, if your cranky farmer friends don't get their sheep dipped within the statutory period, they'll be in serious trouble. They'll be made to pay for breaking the law, I assure you. Actually, I can't understand why *you* should bother with alternate sheep-dip. You're only a locum. Your awkward farmer friends are Phil Brogan's pigeon, not yours.'

'I happen to share their views on BHC pollution.'

'Good God! You haven't grown up, have you? Almost got yourself struck off the register ten years ago, didn't you. If you have forgotten, I haven't. It was Dave Thornton you covered up for, wasn't it? You found out that he'd had his herd immunized against foot and mouth . . . which was totally illegal . . . and you didn't report him. I know, I know . . . there were reasons, why you got away with it, but if I'd had anything to do with it you *wouldn't* have got away

39

with it. Certainly not. I don't know what your interest in alternate sheep-dips is . . . but let me give you one bit of warning. If you step out of line again I'll see you get what's coming to you. And if you know what's good for your cranky sheep-owners you'll tell them to get on with the dipping. Shorty . . . the inspector will be on the spot, I assure you. And if there's *one* sheep not dipped by midnight of 13th November I'll make sure that the law's carried out to the letter.'

The encounter with Dick Craven left a nasty taste behind. All the same it was unwise of me to tell Julia about it in front of her father.

'Red tape,' snorted the colonel. 'Got that kind of thing from the war office. Chairborne types never did understand the problems in the field. Did I ever tell you about that fellah Clutterbuck le Church they sent out to us when I was stationed in India? Forget the year . . . but we were in Jamshedpur . . .'

'Yes, Daddy,' said Julia. 'you have told us.'

Of course the colonel ignored her. While Mrs Cockman's rabbit pie congealed on his plate, he told the story all over again. And when it was finished he launched into other, equally well-known tales of bureaucratic incompetence or bloddy-mindedness.

There was only one way of stemming the flow. I asked father-in-law where his alsation was.

'Biddy? Isn't she here?'

'No, Daddy. Nor in the kitchen.' Julia looked at me, signalling helplessness.

I said, 'Colonel, I wish you'd discipline your bitch.'

'Julia's too old for that.'

'I'm not talking about your daughter. You mustn't let Biddy roam . . . not while you're staying in farming country.'

'She's bound to be with her companion.'

'Who?'

'The collie, old chap . . . what's his name . . . Bachelor.'

40

'Well, I think you should go and look for her.'

'Will do . . . later.'

'Better make it soon.'

'No hurry, old chap. Got to let the lunch go down before I do my yoga exercises.'

'*I'll go*,' said Julia.

'Later,' the colonel lifted a tweedy elbow. 'I've got the leather patches. You promised to sew them on for me.'

I liked my father-in-law. But somehow I was relieved when Mrs Cockman came in and gave me a telephone message. Would I go over to Mr Thornton's farm. One of his animals had hurt itself and he couldn't stop the bleeding.

CHAPTER 5

'Never seen the likes of it.' Dave Thornton, looking queasy, was leaning on the side of a sheep-pen, staring at a large ram whose face was dripping blood. Beyond the pen a hundred or more sheep were being driven – one by one – into a deep concrete bath and from there into a large, hedged-in field.

'What happened to him?' 'Frank and John were trying to get him into the bath...he broke loose and crashed into the post over there. Horn came clean off.'

Two men in heavy protective clothing were manhandling the next sheep into the dip. I could see that Dave was loathing the inevitable violence.

'You know, Michael, sheep are not stupid.'

Obviously not. Each animal in turn was taking evasive action. And yet, when it had been caught and brought to the bath it gave up the struggle. It was as if the sheep knew when they were licked, knew when compliance would save them from accidental injuries.

'Hey, Shorty!' called Dave. 'The vet's here. Will you give us a hand?'

The tall, broad-shouldered young man, who'd been watching beside the bath, came vaulting over the fence. Dave said he was the diseases of animals inspector who'd come to supervise the dipping. 'You don't mind helping us, do you, Shorty? Think you can go in and hold the poor brute steady?'

'Sure.' Shorty beat his hands together. 'It'll warm me up.'

He climbed into the pen. The injured ram, still undefeated, charged. Shorty let him pass and then quitely followed him into the corner. 'Steady boy, steady.' Stroking the ram's neck he murmured reassurance until the animal looked relaxed. 'Okay.'

Dave went in first, taking hold of the ram around the body; I followed with my case. The horn had broken off completely, leaving a hole which was bleeding profusely. And there was blood coming from the nostril on the same side. I reckoned that the scroll-like bone inside the nasal passage had been fractured, damaging its outer covering of mucous membrane. This membrane, being supplied with many blood-vessels, was responsible for the worst bleeding.

I took out a syringe and filled it with a styptic solution, telling Shorty to hold the ram's head in such a position that the solution wouldn't flow into the animals throat. As I don't normally deal with sheep it surprised me that the ram kept so still – as if he knew that the treatment would make him feel better.

The socket of the horn was more worrying. Cauterizing the wound would have been the most effective way of stopping the haemorrhage. But without a general anaesthetic this method would have been too painful. As the wound looked reasonably clean I packed it with a gelatin sponge.

'You can let him go now,' I told Dave and Shorty.

'Should we keep him isolated?' asked Dave.

'I wouldn't.' It was Shorty who answered. 'Put him among the ewes. It'll make him feel more himself.'

'Is that right, Michael?'

'I think Shorty's right,' I agreed. 'Has he been dipped?'

'No.'

'What dip are you using?'

Dave looked at me, a bit warily – I thought. 'BHC,' he said. 'Only dip around.'

'Well then, don't dip him until the wound's healed over.'

'That's all right...We've got another lot of sheep to dip, over at South Meadow. I can put it off for a couple of weeks. All right?'

'I should think so.'

'I'd better get back to the bath,' said Shorty. 'Dave, your men work too fast when I'm not around.'

Thornton laughed. 'Each sheep's supposed to stay immersed for a minute at least...but the minutes are a bit

43

short if the inspector isn't watching.'

'Why aren't you dipping all your sheep in one go?' I asked Dave.

'Tricky business. I guess you know that Tiger's refusing to use BHC. I am – as you might say – compromising; dipping most of my sheep now and leaving about fifty to the last minute...that's in case Tiger does come up with an alternate dip.'

'What's the point?'

'Well...it wouldn't be right to let Tiger fight against BHC all on his own. After all, the St George Clemenses are my neighbours. And I think he's basically right.'

'Then why don't you support him altogether?'

'Can't. I've got to do the dipping when I can get extra hands...We can manage about fifty sheep – the children, Conny and me. But that's all...Besides, one's got to think of the money.'

'The fines?'

'Sure. All right for Tiger...he hasn't got more than twenty sheep. Know what happens if you don't get your animals dipped on time? They might give you three weeks' grace – if you have an excuse. But after that the ministry take you to court and you're fined. If you have up to ten animals the maximum fine is four hundred pounds. If you have more than ten it costs you fifty pounds per amimal. With our flocks it would run into thousands and that we couldn't afford.'

'What would happen if you refused to dip your sheep? ...not that I'd agree with it.'

'They'd fine you until you can no longer afford to pay. In the end you couldn't afford to keep your animals and you'd have to slaughter them. It'll cost Tiger dear if he doesn't come up with an alternate dip which is accepted by Dick Craven.'

'So Dick Craven tells me.'

We walked along to the barn where I'd left the car. The dipped sheep had wandered over the brow of the hill, as far from the loathed bath as possible. Suddenly I saw a large black dog pelt towards the sheep. It looked as if it might harass them, when a collie cut across its path and stopped it dead.

Dave, who'd stiffened, relaxed. 'It's Bachelor and his alsatian bitch again.' He laughed. 'He's training her to become a working sheepdog I reckon.'

'My father-in-law's bitch. He shouldn't let her out.'

'Neither he should. No harm done though, so long as Bachelor's in control... Funny thing, teaching an alsatian bitch sheepcraft.'

Bachelor lay down and gave a high bark. Obediently Biddy turned from the sheep and trotted away, pursued by the collie. I whistled, thinking that I might take her home in the car, but she paid no attention. The two dogs made for the footpath and I gathered that Bachelor was taking Biddy back to her owner before she could break the sheepdog code.

Mrs Cockman was not in the kitchen or the dining room, which reminded me that we were eating with Claire and Tiger. In the lounge father-in-law, dressed in his Japanese kimono, was sitting cross-legged in front of the log fire – doing another stint of yoga, no doubt. Biddy was with him, lying on her back, paws in the air – probably indulging in yoga for dogs. Between the two of them stood the inevitable tumbler of whisky.

'Where's Julia?' I asked.

'We're meditating.' The colonel sounded displeased.

I went to stand beside him, with my back to the fire. The weather had suddenly turned wintery.

'Your wife . . .' the colonel felt for his whisky, 'is upstairs... changing, I expect. We're dining out, I believe.'

Julia was in our bedroom, blow-drying her hair. She looked like one of those obscenely romantic TV adverts for Virgin-bloom Shampoo.

'New dress?' I asked. The yellow did look good with her black hair.

'You're hopeless!' She turned and smiled. 'First of all I've had this outfit three years or more; secondly it isn't a dress...it's a skirt and sweater.'

'It suits you, anyway.'

'Well ... I'd rather wear my red dress, but it wouldn't go with Claire's colours...those awful purple and mustard walls. And I bet she'll wear something to match one of those cats she always drapes over her shoulders.'

'You don't sound happy, Julia.'

'Well ... Have you seen daddy?'

'Downstairs, on the floor.'

'Exactly. I'm not mad about going out with him. He's becoming so eccentric.'

'He always has been.'

'I suppose you're right. Only, when I lived with him I didn't notice. I tried to pin him down today.'

'About going back to Leamington Spa?'

'Yes. After all, this isn't our house. I mean...he's been here more than a week. All I got out of him was, *Biddy's having such a good time with Bachelor.*'

'Then he did give you an answer. He's going to stay here until we leave.'

'I don't know how I'll survive, bless daddy. Here...' Julia took a plate of sandwiches from the dressing table and offered it to me.

'Aren't we eating out?'

'Yes, with Claire and Tiger. That's why I made sandwiches.'

'Wise girl.'

'Do you remember the time they discovered frozen herringballs?'

'Served with half-cooked rice swimming in water.'

Julia giggled. 'And Claire saying that the one thing Tiger cooked well was rice.'

'I want to return the file on sheep-dip to him. Don't let me forget it.'

'I've done some work on it, Michael.'

'You?'

'Look, I know when you're getting involved. I thought

I'd better check on BHC...find out for you whether it *is* as poisonous as Tiger says.'

'So what did you do?'

'Phoned our doctor. He put me on to a pathologist who runs a research unit.'

'Well done.' If I had admitted to myself that the BHC dip worried me, I'd have taken the same action. Now, because of Dick Craven's attitude, I stopped sitting on the fence.

'The pathologist – Dr Owen – phoned back. He said gamma BHC is the same as lindane and he's got a lot of data on lindane as a health hazard. For instance, the smallest dose of lindane that produces a clinical effect is much smaller than that of DDT...Dr Owen's sending you facts and figures...What's going to happen, Michael?'

'We'll see. The dinner at the St George Clemenses won't just be a social get-together.'

As the colonel insisted on driving us to the party in his car we were late. His car never started easily and when it was cold he inevitably had to open the bonnet and fiddle a screw. Outside the St George Clemenses' house my father-in-law shunted the car back and forth, executing a complicated manoeuvre, to make it face the right way for a quick get-away. He'd explained the principle to us more than once; after a convivial evening, possibly with a brandy or two over the odds, it was best to avoid reversing cars. He'd learned his lesson when a brother officer had reversed his car clean through the brigadier's drawing room.

Eventually we got out, covered in Biddy's hairs of course. Claire had come out of her flying saucer house, waiting patiently while the colonel made sure that the boot and all four doors were locked. We were walking along the path to the steps when something came crashing through the shrubs – the biggest sheep I'd ever seen. It came charging at us with a speed that made Julia scream and hurl herself into my arms.

'Baa, no!' called Claire.

Bionic Baa came to a halt so suddenly that she skidded

and came to sit at our feet. She was a remarkably good-looking animal with her thick white fleece, black legs and soulful black face.

'You're a naughty girl.' Claire came down and grabbed Bionic Baa by the scruff. 'I've told you, you mustn't scare people like that...Off you go now.'

Baa rose and lovingly gazed at Claire's face.

'I'm sorry,' apologized our hostess. 'She's absolutely harmless...just like a big, silly dog. But sometimes she does knock people down...We don't really know what to do with her. I hand-reared her and she's got an idea that she has a right to live in the house...Do come in...Baa, no! Not you.'

Baa thought otherwise. She pushed in front of us and walked in through the front door.

'All right,' Claire sighed. 'Go in the kitchen if you must.' She took Julia's coat and put it on a rack made of stag's antlers.

'What a lovely dress,' Julia complimented Claire.

'It's fun, isn't it.' Claire's dress seemed to be made up of purple handkerchiefs, which fluttered at every movement. What with her white stockings and shoes she looked like something designed by Beardsley. 'I got it in the King's Road. You'll never guess where...in one of the antique markets. It was an absolute snip...Only two hundred pounds. Don't you adore getting a bargain?' The lilac-pointed Siamese cat, draped across Claire's shoulder was sharpening her claws on the *bargain*. 'Chang-Ch'ing's tummy's rather upset, or she wouldn't be presenting claws. She must have eaten something nasty...No Chang-Ch'ing! I'm not having this.' She picked the cat off her neck and put it on Bionic Baa's back. 'It's been one of these days.'

The cat arched her back, yawned and lay down on the sheep, partly disappearing in the deep wool. Bionic Baa looked quite happy; her domestic status as the cat's rug confirmed, she followed us into the lounge.

'Darling, couldn't you keep Bionic Baa out?' asked Tiger. 'She takes up rather a lot of room.'

'No way, darling,' said Claire. 'It *is* rather chilly outside.'

Tiger went to the bar, a huge antique globe of the earth, and offered us drinks. Father-in-law immediately made for Madame Shrapnell, who looked luscious in a green see-through dress. The only other guests were Bobby Bowles, in jeans, and Shorty.

'No ill-effects from your fall?' I asked Bobby.

'What happened?' Shorty looked concerned.

'Oh, a lorry worried Badger and he threw me.'

'You didn't tell me.'

'I'm all right. Anyway it happened ages ago. Mr Morton, I am a bit worried about Badger though.'

'Is he limping?'

'No, it isn't that. He makes a funny sort of noise . . . sometimes it sounds like snoring, sometimes it's more of a cough. It doesn't seem to worry Badger, but will you look at him . . . any time you can fit him in.'

'Yes, of course.'

'Let's eat,' said Claire. 'We're having something new.'

The look in Julia's eyes was triumphant. Hadn't she been right making me eat those pre-dinner sandwiches?

Tail and Peter Ford arrived after the grapefruit. It was Peter's fault that they were late – explained Tail, affectionately. He didn't know where to draw the line at spoiling his nephew and niece. Tony and Jill were becoming adept at resisting sleep. That their aunt stayed with them wasn't enough. Night after night they kept Peter talking with them, staying awake even when he tried to knock them out with a school lesson in English or geography. It was understandable – but they were certainly turning Peter into a father substitute. And yet Peter and Jenny were still worried about the children; though they liked listening they were still much too silent and withdrawn – except with Patch. They were holding long conversations with the little mongrel, and Patch was taking advantage of his privileged position . . . sleeping on every bed in the house and chewing up everything below eye-level from shoes to electric flexes.

Tiger and Claire, going back and forth between kitchen

and dining room, had filled the center of the table with bowls of salads which looked perfectly edible. Finally Claire deposited a wooden platter with a Matterhorn-shaped mountain of something soft and reddish brown.

'Looks interesting,' said Mrs Shrapnell. 'Like...like distressed mahogany.'

'Distressed mahogany?' Even Tiger looked puzzled.

'Absolutely spot-on,' said father-in-law. 'I know what the dear lady means. Reference to the *Times* of 28th May... page twenty-two, if my memory serves me correctly. Picture of a chest for duelling pistols, wasn't it? made of distressed mahogany...that's what it said in the *Times*.'

'Colonel, you're wonderful!' said Mrs Shrapnell, her eyes full of admiration. 'I *was* thinking of the duelling pistol chest. It must have been the colour of this...dish. Claire, what is it.'

'It's the game paté. Do you know, I discovered it at the supermarket of all places. Such a find! You'll never guess where it comes from.'

'Not France,' said Mrs Shrapnell, firmly.

'No . . . . Mogadiscio.'

Bobby frowned, 'Algiers?'

'Not far off,' Shorty supported her loyally. 'It's Africa all right.'

'East Africa,' Tiger told us. 'Wonderful how the Third World's developing the frozen foods industry. One must support it, don't you know...Do help yourselves.'

When the platter arrived in front of me I noticed that the bottom of the mountain had been severely undermined. I recognized the unmistakable tooth-marks of a cat. As usual in the St George Clemenses' home Chang-Ch'ing and Min had got to the food before us. I was not the only guest who'd excavated the paté from the opposite side, taking the smallest possible portion.

'Tiger's been frightfully clever with the salads,' Claire told us. 'Not one of them's made of fresh vegetables...frozen chicory from France...'

'Thank you, Colonel,' said Mrs Shrapnell, 'I *will* have

some of this.'

'Frozen beanshoots from China,' continued Claire, 'frozen avocado slices from Israel...What else, darling?'

'Frozen carrots from Portugal and cabbage from Germany.'

'Why don't you use the veg from your garden?' asked Tail.

'Couldn't possibly.' Tiger was emphatic. 'Claire's growing them for the horticultural shows. I mean...she'd never get all the prizes she does if we just ate our vegetables.'

The sheep, with the cat still snoozing on her back, had come pushing in between Tiger and Claire – chin resting on the dinner table.

Father-in-law picked up one of the dishes. 'Surely this celery's fresh.' He was about to offer it to Mrs Shrapnell when Claire almost snatched it from him.

'Actually the celery is from the garden,' she admitted, 'but it's for Bionic Baa.' She selected a stem, but the sheep had other ideas. Somehow Baa managed to get her head under the dish and – as adroit as a footballer – sent it flying across the room where it shattered against Tiger's favourite sculpture. The sculpture, Claire's first ever car flattened into a panel which incorporated beach sandals and cigarette ends, suffered no obvious damage.

With the stage-sense proper to his profession Tiger had set the scene for the real business of the evening in his study. Under the black ceiling, marked with white footprints, enclosed by walls striped mustard and lilac, we flopped into leather sacks filled with bits which felt like gravel but were probably polystyrene. Moving behinds from side to side was all right for youngsters like Tail and Peter or Bobby and Shorty; they'd been brought up on pop and the twist. But for the colonel and Mrs Shrapnell it was not so easy to make tolerable seats out of those floppy leather sacks. Even Julia and I had to do a lot of sliding around before we found positions safe from capsizing.

Claire came in with a tray of tiny cups and a marvellous

antique silver coffee pot – followed by Bionic Baa, who was now accommodating both cats on her back. Tiger relieved her of the tray, swept aside bundles of papers, and put it on his desk.

Claire, he told us, had once again been farsighted and accomplished another housekeeping miracle. Last year she'd harvested the acorns off the oak trees, dried and pulverized them. Now, with coffee costing a scandalous three pounds per pound and more, they had a splendid stock of their homegrown acorn-coffee. Well...it didn't taste like common or garden coffee, but it did have an extraordinarily distinctive flavour. As a matter of fact the boss of a supermarket chain had asked Claire whether she could supply his firm with *acorfee*, to be mixed with the ordinary Kenya coffee. Quite rightly, she'd refused. She'd applied for a patent instead. More business-like to sell a patent to the highest bidder...especially with the price of coffee liable to go up to five pounds per pound.

When we'd mastered the *acorfee*, every one of us declining second helpings, Claire handed round the most expensive peppermints on the market and Tiger sat down on his desk.

'How shall we do it? he asked. 'Perhaps those of you who've done things about an alternate sheep-dip had better tell us the results – if any. Shall I kick off?...Well, I went up to the ministry in London. Took me all day to find the right department. Actually the right department turned out to be a young actress...doing the min job while she's resting...'

'She was absolutely thrilled,' said Claire, 'to meet the author of *Three Brassieres to Bond Street* . . .'

'She was just a nice kid,' Tiger told us, modestly. 'She took me to a sort of store-room full of filing cabinets...'

'Tiger came home covered in cobwebs,' said Claire.

'Yes, it was rather dusty. What she turned up for me was frightfully interesting . . . the past orders for dipping sheep. Apparently dipping was made compulsory in 1928 . . . on 25th January and 6th June, to be precise; then again on 9th January 1930, and yet again on 22nd January and 12th September 1934 . . .'

'Damned fellow Hitler,' father-in-law recalled. '1934 was the year when he was getting too big for his boots. Dare say our animals got the sickness because we imported sheep from Germany . . . trying to pacify the bounder. Period when the Jerries couldn't care less about their agriculture. Goebbels said it . . . the policy was *guns before butter*. Would have saved a lot of trouble if we'd listened to all that *guns before butter* propaganda. I remember . . .'

'Daddy . . . *no*,' sighed Julia. 'You can tell us later.'

'Oh . . . er . . .' The colonel was miffed. 'If you insist.'

'You must tell *me*,' purred Mrs Shrapnell.

'Pleasure, dear lady.'

Tiger picked up a sheet of paper. 'Fascinating information, of course, but rather useless for our purposes. The historic sheep-scab orders didn't specify what the sheep were to be dipped in. Besides, the orders were revoked a long time ago. All rather disheartening I'm afraid.'

There was a silence in which I could hear Bionic Baa's feet tick along the polished floor.

'Well . . .' Bobby looked about her. 'I haven't got anything definite . . . but my father's promised to hold off dipping our sheep until 15th November . . .'

'And we've got the same promise from other farmers,' said Tail. 'Dave's already used BHC but he's keeping back some of our sheep. Willis, McNab and Standing say they're going to wait until Monday week. If, by then, we've found an alternate dip they're not going to order BHC.'

'That's good.' Tiger didn't sound too convinced.

'I,' said Mrs Shrapnell, 'sat down in the street . . . with all my dogs.'

'Whatever for?' asked father-in-law.

'In front of the ministry vet's offices. Nowadays one has to make a demonstration or no one pays attention. Mr Dick Craven and his staff were forced to hold up the traffic and scrape us off the street . . . We resisted, of course.'

'I know,' Shorty laughed. 'I picked up Tommy. That old

spaniel's a real heavyweight . . .'

'In my opinion the demo was worthwhile,' Mrs Shrapnell assured us. 'While Dick Craven was trying to drag me off, I presented him with a petition against BHC signed by fifty people. And this week there'll be more petitions . . . from the Surrey Wild Life Association and the Royal Rabbits Jubilee Society for the Protection of the British Rabbit.'

'Anyone else?' asked Claire.

I said, 'Julia's been in touch with a London research outfit. They're going to send us data on BHC as a health hazard.'

'Knew I could count on you two,' Tiger thanked us.

'I also went up to London,' said Shorty.

'Chatting up birds . . .' murmured Bobby.

'Sure . . . the farmyard Casanova, that's me. I met a bird all right; she was in my year at agricultural college. We talked shop at lunch, in a pub. She hates living in London, so I promised I'd help find her a job down here.' Shorty took a notebook from his pocket. 'Here's the dope she gave me . . . There are no less than three sheep-dips – other than BHC – which are approved by the ministry: lime and sulphur; carbolic acid and soft soap; and tobacco and sulphur . . .'

'The breakthrough, darling!' Claire squeezed Tiger's arm. 'I knew it! I knew we'd win.'

'Not yet, darling,' said Tiger soberly. 'Shorty, do you know the formula for these dips?'

'Anna turned up the quantities required to make up a hundred gallons of sheep-dip.'

'Good. Where can one get the ingredients?'

'That mightn't be so easy. Where – for a start – would one buy thirty-five pounds of finely ground offal tobacco without paying tobacconists' prices? I think we'll have to scrub the tobacco and sulphur mix and try for the others. Trouble is, even for them we need large quantities of nasty chemicals . . . the kind manufacturers normally sell direct to industrial customers or to chemists and no one else. But Anna gave me a few addresses of small firms who might let us have the stuff. So far I've phoned three of them; one's gone out of business, one's changed from dealing in sulphur and carbolic to making face creams; the third,' Shorty consulted his notes, 'firm called Leo Lemming Ltd. . . . well, the man I talked to sounded like Billy Graham; he gave me a lecture on Jesus Christ.'

'How many more have you got there?' asked Tiger.

'Cruickshank Chemicals . . . they're near Havant . . . and Sidney Franks Associates.'

'That's funny,' said Julia and her father in unison.

'Michael,' Julia managed to get first. 'Sidney Franks . . . he wouldn't be the crook who was mixed up with the racing gang . . .?'

'The horse-doping gang, you mean.' I certainly remembered that spot of trouble and – no less – Sidney conning Dave Thornton into buying his illegal vaccine against foot-and-mouth. I said, 'I wouldn't mind investigating Sidney Franks Associates.'

'Right, you're on,' agreed Tiger. 'But remember, we don't care about the past. What we want's the chemicals, now.'

'As I was saying,' the colonel spoke up, 'Funny thing . . . Leo Lemming rings a bell. Can't be two chaps with that name. Had a batman in the war, name of Leo Lemming. Always on the take, but there was nothing he couldn't procure for his friends; you name it . . . rationed food, electric heaters, cigars, brandy. Never did find out how he managed it. Always talked himself out of clink. Bounced back to me like a bad penny. Keen on the church . . . as Mr Shorty said, talking his head off about Jesus Christ.'

'Oh, Colonel,' breathed Mrs Shrapnell, 'I'd love to know whether Leo Lemming Ltd and your batman's the same person.'

'Easy, dear lady. 'We'll go and find out, if you'd care to accompany me.'

'I really would. Thank you, Colonel.'

'Where does the chap hang out?' asked father-in-law.

'London . . . Paddington,' said Shorty.

'Well, I'm sure we'll enjoy the drive.'

'You can enjoy the drive, Daddy,' snapped Julia. '*We* will see to the chemicals.'

Tiger went to a wall cupboard and brought out a huge bottle of Spanish brandy. 'Nightcap everyone? Right. That's settled then. With Dave and other farmers hanging on for the non-BHC dips we'll be needing enough to make quite a few hundreds of gallons, won't we? So I suggest we do our shopping at all the firms. We can decide on our regular supplier next year.' He tipped brandy into purple pottery goblets. 'Colonel, you'll go up to Leo Lemming Ltd?'

'Pleasure.'

'Michael and Julia . . . You'll try Sidney Franks?'

'Right.'

'Who wants to do Cruikshank Chemicals?'

'I will,' promised Bobby.

'You only took your driving test last week,' objected Shorty.

'I passed, didn't I.'

'All right; I'll come for the ride.'

'We'd have to go in business hours.'

'I'll manage . . . don't worry.'

Claire passed us the goblets. She was giving one to the colonel when Bionic Baa nudged her and made her spill the brandy. The sheep immediately put out her tongue and mopped it up.

'It's my fault,' said Claire. 'When Baa was a little lamb she was so weak that I used to give her brandy in her milk.'

Tiger smiled. 'She's been knocking it back ever since.'

Bionic Baa was butting Claire more demandingly.

Tiger went out and returned with a dish.

'No,' Claire objected. 'She's not going to have any more brandy. Do you realise what this brandy costs nowadays? Besides, I can't get it anywhere except in Fortnums.'

'Anything you say.' Tiger put the dish on his desk. 'I just wanted to save you from getting bruised again.'

We were talking about when and where we could brew up the sheep-dip, sipping brandy, when we heard a dog bark outside – the unmistakable deep bark of Biddy.

'Daddy, you promised to lock her in . . . You mustn't let her roam around Craftly by night.' Julia heaved herself out of the leather bag. 'I'll get her.'

The colonel shook his head. 'You're always fussing . . . becoming more and more like your mother, Julia. Biddy's got a perfectly good sheepdog looking after her . . . Perhaps our dear hostess would like one of the pups?'

'Kind of you, Colonel.' Claire rubbed her hip, where Baa had just butted her. 'Perhaps when the sheep are off our minds . . .'

On the morning after I wakened early, a somewhat tender feeling in my head reminding me of Tiger's Spanish brandy. At the same time I remembered that I hadn't asked where Sidney Franks Associates were trading in chemicals. It had occurred to Tiger too. He phoned the address while we were at breakfast; it was at Pontefract, no small distance from Craftly.

If Sidney was our old horse-doper he wouldn't answer a letter. When I phoned him from the surgery I immediately recognized the voice. Pitching my own an octave higher, I introduced myself as Farmer Bill Budd of Ardingly, Sussex. Yes, Sidney confirmed, he could let me have the chemicals I required. If I sent him my cheque he'd send the goods by rail.

'It would be better for me to pick the stuff up at the weekend,' I told him. I wasn't going to risk Tiger's money on an advance payment.

'Weekends is a bit difficult, guv,' said Sidney.

'Never mind. I'll go to another firm.'

'You want them chemicals fresh, don't you?' The whine was familiar too. 'Other firms isn't that reliable, if you take my meaning, guv. Now, if you come on the Saturday . . .'

'Late afternoon?'

'Suits me. I'll have the stuff all ready for you, guv.'

'Don't parcel it up, Mr Franks.' I'd certainly take a good

look at the containers. 'I might want more.'

'Please yourself, guv. If I'm out, me personal assistant – gent by the name of Bobo – will look after you. If you pay cash he'll give you a discount.'

If anyone had told me ten years ago that I'd be pleased to come across Sidney and his boyfriend again I certainly wouldn't have believed it. Yet now, the memory of Bobo feeding lobster to his tropical fish or dancing to ear-splitting pop music made me feel quite nostalgic.

CHAPTER 6

'Thought I'd look in for a minute.' Dick Craven closed the surgery door behind him.

His half-smile, whether or not meant as a peace-offering, didn't impress me. He'd remembered something less than comfortable from my past, and he'd threatened me. I said, '*Looking in* isn't done in the middle of a surgery.' Perhaps I should have told him to get out and wait.

He sat down beside the instrument cabinet, apparently unperturbed, and I continued emptying the anal gland of a very old little Yorkshire terrier. The stink of it was overpowering, worrying the old lady who owned the dog less than the ministry vet.

The job completed, I took my time, making a fuss of the terrier. Picking him up, I told him that he was a plucky little fellow and gave him a dog chocolate drop. It was much appreciated by old Miss Byrnes, the few minutes of bedside manner giving her time to recover from the trauma of holding the dog during treatment.

'When will it need cleaning out again?' she asked me.

'I think you'll be the best judge of that. Miss Byrnes . . . You're able to tell, aren't you?'

'I knows by the look and smell of it, doctor. But I put it off. It's not nice for Tiggy.'

'More comfortable for him if you don't put it off.'

'I won't then, doctor. What do I owe you?'

'Nothing.'

'Mr Brogan wouldn't 'old with that.'

'Never mind. You'll be paying next time.'

'Thank you, doctor. . .it'll be fifty pence then.'

'Right,' Craven got up. 'That was your last patient . . . and a nice bit of public relations work at that.'

'I don't believe in soaking old age pensioners.' Stupid,

allowing myself to be drawn. 'What do you want?'

'A word about those brewed-up sheep-dips some of your friends are intending to use.'

'Well?' I couldn't imagine Shorty, that decent diseases of animals inspector, reporting us to Dick Craven.

'Viscount St George Clemens informed me . . .'

Not a bad idea to give fair warning. No one wanted a come-back from the ministry. 'I expect he mentioned that these non-BHC dips are approved by your boss in London.'

'He did, Morton; he did. And you're perfectly entitled to using these dips . . . that's if you can get the ingredients in time. My department, on the other hand, has the clear duty to test such rather home-made dips more rigorously than the normal BHC baths.'

'Is that another one of your threats?'

'Just a warning to your cranks that I will not accept dips which have been over-diluted with water. They'd better be very meticulous . . . but then, I assume that the dipping will be carried out under your personal supervision.'

There was no reason why any farmer should pay a vet for attending the sheep-dipping. Whether I would attend, on a friendly basis, would finally depend on the amount of work in the practice. I wasn't rushed at the moment, but that could change any day – as I'd learned from earlier stints in country practices.

That afternoon I had two calls which reminded me of the kind of incidents which could suddenly catapult a vet into a period of sixteen-hour working days. One was from Claire; Bionic Baa had gone listless and shivery. Immediately after, Conny Thornton phoned; Dave had lost one of his best ewes and two others seemed unwell.

As Bionic Baa was probably suffering no worse than a hangover, I went to the Thorntons' first.

Dave took me to the back of the winter pens and showed me the carcass of a good looking Southdown ewe. 'She was all right yesterday, Michael. I know, because I fed her the concentrates myself. Today we were taking the ewes – the flock that's due for lambing before Christmas – under cover, and she was left behind . . . dead. Just like that. Never had that happen before . . . not since I went into sheep. We've been looking all over for poison plants; didn't find a thing . . . we got rid of hemlock and cowbane years ago. What do you think? What could have done it?'

'I've seen your sheep drink from the little stream.'

'That's always been clean.'

'Something could have got into the water, I suppose.'

'The BHC dip?'

'It's possible, isn't it?'

Dave shook his head. 'We emptied all the used dip into a specially dug soak-away . . . I didn't think it could get through into the brook.'

'It probably didn't. I wouldn't put the blame on BHC.'

'What then.'

'Let me see the sick sheep before we jump to conclusions.'

Dave took me into the roofed winter quarters, to the pens at the end, where he'd isolated a couple of Southdowns which were trembling like wet dogs. They were also abnormally restless, lying down and rising frequently.

'It could be an enterotoxaemia,' I told Dave.

'What's that?'

'Difficult to say. The symptoms are similar but the disease can have different causes . . . from bacterial infections to the absorption of a chemical breakdown product . . .'

'So it *is* BHC.'

'No, Dave, the chemical reaction would happen inside the animal's body due to helminth infestation.'

'Worms?'

'That's right.'

'I'd have noticed worms before now.'

'Well, a bacterial infection's more likely.'

'Are we going to lose them?'

'Hope not . . . I'll give them an injection . . .'

Dave watched me fill a syringe with sulphamezathine.

Holding each ewe in turn, while I gave the injections, he talked to his animals much as I'd heard him talk to his children. He wouldn't go until the animals had quietly settled on their straw.

'Anything else we should do?' he asked, following me out.

'It might be wise to vaccinate all sheep which have been in contact with the sick ones . . . That means two lots of injections, serum and pulpy kidney vaccine.'

'Right; that's what I want you to do, Michael.'

'I suppose the dead animal was in the same flock.'

'Yes.'

'Then the surest way of getting the correct diagnosis would be to take the dead one to the veterinary investigation centre . . . for a *post mortem.*'

'I don't want to lose any more of my animals. Could you arrange a *post mortem?*'

'I will, Dave.'

He dug his fists into the pockets of his anorak. 'It's bitter. Come in for a cup of tea.'

The house, which had been comfortably cool when Julia and I had stayed with the Thorntons in the tropical summer, was now invitingly warm. The kitchen, with the waxed oak furniture that Dave's father had made, smelled of baking bread and the log fire.

'You should have brought Julia,' Conny welcomed me. She was a tall girl, unlike her sister Tail, but beside Dave she looked almost frail.

'Julia's father's staying with us. He needs a bit of looking after.'

Conny laughed. 'So does his alsatian, I hear.' She put one of the freshly baked loaves on the table. 'Though Tiger's sheepdog's attending to her.'

'Has my father-in-law been trying to sell you the future pups?'

'Not yet.' Conny put the water into the familiar brown teapot. 'They might be good pups at that.'

Half-way through tea Tail came clattering in.

'You shouldn't . . .' Conny began.

'I know, sister.' Tail still had that well-remembered schoolgirl grin. 'I *haven't* been driving in my platform shoes. I take them off.'

'Tea?'

'No time. Got a rehearsal.'

'You must eat, Tail.'

'Always do. Stuff myself like a pig. Midnight raids on your larder. Bye all.'

'She'll never grow up.' Conny smiled, listening to the thunder of those platform shoes above our heads.

Inevitably we returned to the subject of sheep. Dave, still feeling somewhat guilty for not giving full support to Tiger's anti-BHC campaign, explained his timetable. He'd put out his rams in the middle of July so that the ewes should be lambing between the middle of December and the end of January. For most of his sheep he'd had to use BHC because the dipping had to be carried out at least a month before lambing. Now he'd gone into the final care of the ewes, feeding them concentrates of oats, dried distillers' grains, cotton cake and bran.

'We've been expecting about fifteen hundred lambs,' he said, miserably. 'Now . . . with this bug that's making them sick . . .'

'Dave's always looking on the black side,' said Conny. 'It's not that bad, Michael, is it?'

'I don't think so . . . Dave, get the contracts together. I'll vaccinate them tomorrow. Know how many there'll be?'

'No more than eighty . . . but that'll be enough for you.'

It didn't take an expert to see that Bionic Baa's case was different. Nothing like the symptoms I'd observed in Dave's sheep. Bionic Baa was wandering around the lounge, bright-eyed, friendly and on the scrounge.

'After we phoned you,' said Claire, 'Tiger gave her a lot of sugar . . . just in case she was suffering from a hang-over.'

'It seems to have worked. You shouldn't give her food at

63

the table; certainly not brandy.'

'It's difficult,' said Tiger. 'Bionic Baa demands things rather forcefully. She's such a positive person.'

'She's a sheep, not a person,' I told them brutally.

'Well,' Tiger smiled. 'My advice to you is . . . never hand-rear a little lamb, because little lambs become big indoor pets . . . Out there is a luxurious home, specially built for Bionic Baa; heated of course. She's never spent a night in it . . . she lets it to lodgers.'

'To be more practical,' I ignored Baa, who'd put her head on my lap – to be scratched behind the ears, presumably. 'What about the rest of your sheep. Have you had them immunized against pulpy kidney disease?'

'Masters gets all animals immunized against everything,' said Claire. 'We'll ask him.'

'And let me know.'

'Of course, if you wish. Is it because Dave's lost a sheep?'

'Yes. But it's a sensible precaution in any case.'

On my way home, driving through flurries of snow, I began to see what I was letting myself in for. If Dave Thornton, perhaps the best farmer in the district, had missed out on immunizing his flocks, how many more farmers owned animals vulnerable to pulpy kidney disease? It was just one of the things I hadn't considered when I'd agreed to do a locum for Phil Brogan. Now, for a start, I'd have to go through the whole of Phil's card index. If he was running his practice efficiently – and I believed that he was – he'd have a note on the immunization programme of every farm on his list whose owner observed modern husbandry practices.

Though I was due to finish my work in Craftly in two weeks' time, it would be wrong to ignore routine obligations and leave him a backlog. In fact, he'd have every right to complain if I neglected the established commitments of the practice in favour of the anti-BHC issue. Nothing I'd read about BHC commended it to me, yet I was well aware that years would pass before the ministry would acknowledge the disadvantages of BHC and finally recommend or adopt a less polluting sheep-dip.

Yes, the change would be a long time coming. Yet *someone* had to start revolutions, especially scientific and humane ones. It was me who had to get my priorities right; and as far as I could see that meant doing all of Phil Brogan's work, without cutting corners, plus finding the time for helping Tiger produce the alternate sheep-dip within the statutory period. I could have done without Dick Craven breathing down my neck and I wished I'd dealt with him more diplomatically.

The V.I. department's report on Dave's dead sheep proved that death had been caused by a bacterial toxin, which meant that my treatment of the sick animals had been right. Dave was not going to lose them.

By Friday night, I had carried out all necessary immunizations for Dave and several neighbouring farmers, working all hours, getting frozen to the bone and dead tired. Getting to bed at one in the morning I was almost looking forward to the long drive to Pontefract.

Julia and I left at six. As she had foreseen, her father's trip with Mrs Shrapnell had not produced results – at least, not the required results. Leo Lemming *had* turned out to be his former batman and they'd celebrated their reunion so enthusiastically that the colonel hadn't even remembered to ask whether Lemming could supply the chemicals we needed. Nor could the colonel recall whether he'd spent the night at Lemming's or Mrs Shrapnell's house and whether or not he'd asked Mrs Shrapnell to marry him. Since then he'd considered it advisable to stay at home, await an enlightening phone call from Mrs Shrapnell, and let Bachelor supervise Biddy's excursions into the countryside.

It had been Julia's idea that we should leave earlier than planned. If we were able to buy the dip ingredients at Lemming's in London we'd save ourselves a long drive, if not we'd go straight on to Pontefract. When we'd phoned Lemming he had been vague but not discouraging.

Julia reckoned we'd be back in Craftly by mid-day.

Hadn't her father said that there was nothing Leo Lemming couldn't procure for his friends? I was less optimistic. Sulphur was a common enough mineral substance, and carbolic acid was used in the manufacture of a wide range of products. And yet Shorty had already discovered that neither was readily available in *small* quantities.

The Havant suppliers he'd approached had blamed *modern times* and metrication. Nowadays there were no end of products one couldn't sell in small lots. Up to five years ago Cruikshank Chemicals would have had no problem selling a few quarts of carbolic acid. But now, what with VAT and the computer breaking down every time it was asked to work out small sums, the obstacles to retail selling had become insuperable. Cruikshank Chemicals had advised Shorty to look for a firm which was not yet computerized.

If the colonel was to be believed, Leo Lemming was an old soldier who'd resist computerization to the end of his days.

CHAPTER 7

We had no problem finding the Paddington street the Colonel had visited, but we'd never have found the alley where Leo Lemming Ltd hung out if an obliging barrow-boy hadn't direct us. Rewarding the leathery little man, we bought bananas and a box of dates from him.

The battered brown door of number 3B was answered by a middle-aged peroxide blonde who smelled of stale perfume and wore the highest platform-soled shoes I'd ever seen. 'Yes?' she asked, cautiously.

I said, 'We're looking for Leo Lemming Ltd.'

'Yes?'

'Is this the right address?'

'Well . . . it's Sa'urday.'

'We made an appointment.'

'Wif Mr Lemming?'

'That's right.'

'I knows nuffing 'bout that.'

'Are you his secretary?'

'Me, I'm Mrs Lemming.'

'That accounts for it.' Julia gave the woman a charming smile. 'Wives are always the last to find out what their husbands are up to.'

'You can say that again,' responded Mrs Lemming, warmly. 'Leo ain't in, see. But I'll tell yer 'ow to find 'im . . . Go out the way you came and turn right in Star Street. You'll see a barrow wif bananas and dates . . .'

'Yes, we bought some.'

'That's it then.'

'Sorry?'

'The barrow-boy. That's 'im . . . Mr Leo Lemming – bloody-Ltd.'

'Colonel 'anley . . . 'e was one of the best.' The elderly

67

barrow-boy was grinning from ear to ear. 'Only orficer we 'ad what never arsked questions when I got 'im a bit of somethin' on the side . . . French brandy, 'avanna cigars-. . . No trouble; 'e paid up and never arsked no questions. That's what I calls businesslike.'

Julia wasn't too happy. It was bitterly cold at the barrow; besides, stories about her father always did make her cringe. 'It was all a long time ago,' she muttered.

'I remember like it was yesterday,' Lemming assured her, 'even me 'olding you in me arms when you was a baby, Miss Julia. Know something? it was me what used to teach you words. Clever little thing she was,' he assured me. 'One day – in India it was – she was lying in 'er cot and I says to 'er . . . pointing to me arm like . . . *what's this? Arm,* she says. *What's this then?* I arsk 'er. *Hand,* she says, quick as a flash. So I shows 'er me fingers . . . *and what's this? Dirt,* she says . . . *dirt* . . . would you believe it?'

Even Julia laughed. All the same, her sense of timing didn't let her down. 'Mr Lemming . . . as my husband told you on the phone . . . we want to do business with you.'

'Pleasure, Miss Julia. Sulphur and carbolic acid, is it? Nasty stuff, if you arsk me.'

'Not as nasty as other chemicals used in preventing a certain disease in sheep,' I told him. 'Now, can you sell us . . .'

'Sorry guv,' he shook his head. 'Don't deal in them chemicals any more. Fact is, I given up all me companies, 'cept one. Know why? Effing government don't believe in private enterprise. Drive us clean out of business . . . 'ard-working blokes like me. Know what made me give up me companies? Last year it was . . . the registrar of companies made me fill up a form . . . eight pages it was; twenty quid 'e charged me just for giving 'im the information as 'ow I own fifty-one shares and me missus forty-nine shares in an 'undred quid company. Makes the angels weep, don't it? Mind you, I'm still a company director . . . barrow-boys 'as got to be company directors; it's what's expected of you in the trade. But in this 'ere trade . . .' he swept an arm across the bananas and dates, 'the tax office can't keeep tabs on you, like they does when you're trading in deadly poisons, see.'

'Yes . . . well, perhaps you could tell us . . .'

Lemming ignored Julia's interruption. 'That's a labour government for you . . . If you're a Lord Snooks and you owe the Inland Revenue a few million pounds they don't worry you . . . years they sits and 'ope your grandson will pay up arter you're dead an' gone. It's different for the likes of me. You bet! Give 'em the chance and they'd soon 'ave the shirt off me back. Don't count that I served me country in its darkest hour . . . The colonel will tell you as 'ow I did, but that's all the thanks you get.'

'It's a shame,' murmured Julia.

'One of the best, is the colonel . . . Nuffin I wouldn't do for 'im.'

'That's why he sent us to you.' Julia was quick off the mark. 'He said if there was anyone who could get us those chemicals it would be you.'

'There you 'ave me.' Lemming shook his head. 'Like I said . . . me company's gone. Now, if you arsked me for a few thousand cut-price cigarettes or some quality transistor radios . . . Tell you what, guv. Why don't you buy Miss Julia a nice mink coat. Coupla hundred quid for you. Cost you two thousand in the shops. Two 'undred cash and Bob's your uncle.'

'We haven't got that kind of cash on us,' said Julia. 'But may be . . .'

'You'll be back?'

'Perhaps . . . when my husband hasn't got things on his mind. He's got to have the chemicals. If you could . . . remember who your supplier was it might save us a long journey.'

'You'd look smashing in the mink.' Lemming was as single-minded as Julia. 'Guv, 'ow about buying it for the wife . . . for Christmas.'

'Well . . . first things first.'

'I don't know whether the firm's still in business, guv.

69

Even when I used to deal with them they didn't always deliver the goods. Funny bloke 'e was.'

I thought I was getting the drift. 'You mean Indian . . . or Ugandan?'

'If it had been one of them I'd 'ave got me deliveries regular like . . . never 'ave no trouble with them. No guv, that bloke was a Londoner, like meself. Mad keen on 'orses, 'e is. Got in trouble racing in the south so 'e upped and went into business in the north.'

I said, 'It's got to be Sidney Franks.'

Lemming grinned. 'Been around, guv, 'ave you! Me, I didn't say nuffin, did I?'

The long-standing barter arrangement, in which I looked after the whippets of a breeder while her husband maintained our old TR2, worked as infallably as ever. Bashing up the M1 we saw quite a few broken-down cars, most of them much newer than ours, while the TR2 purred on like a pampered cat.

Not stopping for a meal, feeding on the bananas and dates, we made Pontefract shortly after two in the afternoon. The beautiful old market town with its mediaeval houses and stone roofs caused Julia a change of heart – temporarily at least. Why did we take so many holidays abroad? she asked. What was the point of gawping at foreign landscapes and buildings when there was so much undiscovered magnificence on our doorstep, in our own country?

'You kept telling me that holidays abroad are good for the children,' I reminded her. 'Educational.'

'Rubbish. *You* like water-skiing and lying in the sun.'

'Me? I peel like a snake. I'd just as soon play golf in Scotland . . . or Pontefract.'

'Golf! That's why we've had to go abroad . . . All the same, next summer we'll stay here.'

'In Pontefract?'

'Yes.' Julia stopped in front of a palatial Chinese restaurant. 'Obviously, it's got everything. Michael, I'm hungry.'

'Want to go in?'

'Yes . . . I bet you it's open.'

It was. A Chinese with a Yorkshire accent allocated us a window table with a pleasant view over a park. After we'd chosen the Cantonese dishes he asked us whether we'd like rice or chips with our meal. Julia turned up her nose at the very idea of eating chips with Chinese food, but our waiter had no inhibitions about serving his Pontefract customers – mostly young couples – large bowls of fried potatoes.

Unlike Mr Lemming's, Sidney Franks's business address was not hard to find. It was a good stone terrace house with pale blue painted woodwork and a smart brass plate, *Sidney Franks Associates. Purveyors.* There was no indication *what* the firm purveyed, furnished or supplied, which didn't surprise me.

The doorbell, a genteel chime, was answered immediately by Sidney in person. He recognized us and adroitly rearranged his rubbery actor's face from dismay to pleasure.

'Good afternoon, Sidney,' Julia greeted him. 'We've come to pick up the order for sulphur and carbolic.'

'Well!' He had the nerve to peck her cheek. 'What an unexpected pleasure! Come in . . . come in.'

He led us into a lounge in which everything was pink – walls and curtains, carpet and armchairs; even the record player and TV set. From a pink velvet couch rose Bobo – in tight jeans and pink sweater.

'Bobo dear, you remember Michael and Julia Morton, don't you?' asked Sidney. 'Julia and I were great friends when she worked at the Purple Pigeon . . . before she married my vet friend of course. What an artiste she was! But all that was before your time.'

'Did I have the tropical fish when you met me?' asked Bobo.

'You did.' Julia looked a little sick.

'I don't go in for them any more. Stupid things. I used to watch them eat each other, but I got bored with it.' He got up, ducked behind the couch and came out with a squirming garter snake.

71

'What a pet!' Julia took it and cradled it in her hands. 'There, there . . . stay with auntie. Aren't you beautiful!'

'Good!' Sidney burst out laughing. 'Great! Bobo boy . . . didn't expect this, did you? Girl who doesn't scream her head off at the sight of your snakes.'

'You like snakes?' asked Bobo, sulkily.

'I absolutely adore them,' Julia assured him.

Bobo flung himself into a chair and retreated into some world of his own.

'Funny boy,' said Sidney, 'but I've got used to him. He's got quite a good business brain. Have a drink?'

'We haven't got much time,' I told him. 'What I want is thirty-six pounds of sulphur and six quarts of carbolic acid. The acid's got to contain not less than ninety-seven per cent of real tar acid. Can you let me have that?'

'I've got to ask what you want it for.'

'Don't you know?' I bluffed. 'It's for making sheep-dip, of course.'

'No one up here's been asking for it.'

'Perhaps they're behind the times. Too traditional. In the south we're giving up BHC in favour of the more harmless dips.'

'Oh . . . well . . . they are a funny lot up here. I'll take you to the store then.' He took a bunch of keys from a drawer of his desk and led us to the back of the hall, out into a yard.

The big shed at the far end was crammed with shelves of weed-killers, flower seeds, small horticultural implements, drums and carboys.

'Good business?' I asked Sidney.

'Can't complain.'

'Racing up north isn't bad either, is it?'

He looked at me sideways. 'Mugs' game; gave it up years ago.'

'That win at Doncaster . . .'

His eyes lit up, 'London Express . . . great horse. It sure wasn't the bookies' day . . . Well, what I mean . . . I saw it on TV. Haven't been to the races since you warned me off.'

'Friend of mine saw you on the course.' It was a shot in the dark.

He looked scared. 'Mr Morton, what is it you want from me?'

'Just the sulphur and carbolic . . . *unadulterated.*'

'I wouldn't give you anything but the best. Wouldn't be sensible; now would it?'

'No, Sidney, it wouldn't.'

'Here we are then.' He stopped before some labelled containers. 'Bobo'll pack up your lot good and safe. He'll take it to the car for you; give you time for a drink.'

'A quick coffee would be nice,' agreed Julia.

'One more thing,' I decided to risk another long shot. 'I'd like the address of your suppliers in London.'

'Leo Lemming Ltd. But they've just gone out of business.'

'I know.'

'Well . . . Tell you what, Mr Morton; mate of mine in Shoreditch looks after the smaller customers. I'll give you his address.'

'It wouldn't be out of date?'

'Never. It's an old family firm.'

'Reputable?'

'Micky? He's as honest as the day is long. Never been inside. No one'll ever pin anything on Micky, take my word for it.'

By Sunday morning I had positive proof that Sidney Franks wanted me out of his life again – a phone call from Micky of Shoreditch, telling me that any friend of Sid's was a friend of his and that he'll be happy to send supplies of sulphur and carbolic to my farmer mates. We now had enough ingredients for dipping Dave's remaining sheep, and Tiger's. If any of the other farmers wanted to use the alternative dip they'd be able to get their supplies quite fast from Micky.

After breakfast I went to the Bowles' farm to take a look at Badger. It was a cold day but the hoarfrost in the hedgerows sparkled in the sun and the young people of the village were out walking on Craftly Beacon. I saw Hugo and his fox and stopped the car.

'How's Custer?'

'He's stopped biting his paw. He hates the stuff you prescribed.'

'Good.'

'Trouble is he hates me too . . . more than before, sulky brute. Never mind . . . in a week or so I'll be allowed to return to normal duties. Think I've just about convinced the big cheese that we're wasting taxpayers' money on Custer.'

'What will you do with him?'

'Turn him loose.'

'Wouldn't a zoo be . . .'

'No.' Hugo was emphatic. 'Don't you worry about Custer, Mr Morton. He'll have no trouble finding a home. There's a vixen waiting for him at the backdoor.'

Bobby was in the yard, unsaddling her pony. She told me she'd had him out on a long ride and he'd given no sign of broken wind until they'd got into the High Street. 'Then he started making this funny noise again . . . a bit like a cough and a wheezing.'

'Any heavy traffic about?'

'Well, there was a container truck . . . one of these big continental things. But he didn't go fast.'

'Whereabouts did Badger begin to cough?'

'Funny you should ask . . . It was at the Craftly Arms, where he fell the other day.'

'Let's take him into his box.'

Badger's chest sounded clear, he had no temperature and he looked fit. I don't think I'd have known what to do about that sporadic cough if I hadn't remembered Herakles, the racehorse which had preferred the Russian jockey to his own.

'What's the matter with Badger?' Bobby had watched me examine her pony and she was looking worried.

'He could be allergic to heavy traffic.'

'Allergic? Like people who can't have a cat in the house . . . or eat certain things?'

'That's it.'

'What are we going to do? I was going to ride him in the horse show next year.'

'He isn't ill, but he'll probably need treatment from time to time. Nothing complicated. I think an occasional injection will do the trick; an antihistamine.'

'Isn't that what you give people? My mother used to get injections . . . She was allergic to pollen.'

'Yes, I'm giving Badger the same kind of thing.'

'What will we do when you're gone?'

'I'll leave a note for Phil Brogan on the farm card.'

'Will it be all right for me to exercise Badger?'

'Of course. You've got to get him ready for the horse show. Now, stop worrying Bobby. Badger's not an invalid.'

'Neither was my mother.' She'd started giving Badger his rub-down. 'But she died.'

'Not of her allergy.' What else could I say?

The pony had turned his head and was nuzzling Bobby's hair. 'It was cancer.'

'Was it the first time you lost someone close to you?'

She nodded. 'Badger was born that day.'

'It's your answer . . . That day people who were important to someone, and animals, died and others were born.'

She looked up, unshed tears in her eyes.

'Bobby, death is a part of life . . . not to be resented. If you accept the pleasures and troubles of every passing day, as you obviously do, you must accept that a time must come when life – as you know it – will change into something else . . . death, for want of a better name.'

'If I knew what happens after death . . . Mr Morton, do you believe in God?'

'Not in the old gentleman with white whiskers. But some great spirit – beyond human imagination – *has* made the universe.'

'Shorty says I should go to church. But I don't like sermons that don't mean anything.'

'Neither do I. Do you know when I learned about these things? When I used a good microscope and looked for the first time at a minute culture . . . tiny organisms. These specks were so superbly well organized that I couldn't believe that the life in them was an accident . . .'

'I see what you mean.' Bobby went back to rubbing down her pony.

'Shorty must be in touch with a veterinary investigation laboratory.'

'I think he is.'

'Why don't you ask him to take you there. They'd let you look through the microscope at slides . . . or just a drop of water.'

'I'd like that . . . Thanks Mr Morton.'

In the afternoon I was reading the *Veterinary Record,* Julia a novel, when Tail and Peter came in with the children and Patch. It was Mrs Cockman's day off, but she'd left us shortbread biscuits and a ginger cake.

We had tea around the big log fire. The colonel was out, presumably with Mrs Shrapnell, and Biddy was sitting right inside the inglenook looking like a Copenhagen china dog. Patch, white front paws on the floor, feathery ears up, was trying to undermine her dignity but Biddy wouldn't play.

'We've got the lime for the lime and sulphur dip,' Tail told us, 'and drums to put it in when it's brewed. And we've got the soft soap for the carbolic and soap dip. What we still need is a boiler that'll take at least a hundred gallons . . . Nobody we've asked has got one, except the antique shop in Nether Craftly.'

'How much do they want for it?'

'Three hundred pounds. It's copper . . . Uncle Michael, there used to be a big boiler in the basement here. Do you think we could borrow it?'

'I don't see why not, if it's still there.'

'It is,' Julia told us, 'beside the wine rack.'

'Good. We've got a concrete shed . . . a left-over of Conny's piggery. Dave says we can light the fire in there . . . we'll put firebricks under the boiler . . . Could we see it?'

'After tea,' Peter smiled at Tail. 'Has she always been a bulldozer?'

'Yes,' I told him, 'even when she was twelve and wanted to become an actress . . . First time I saw Tail she was balancing on the garden wall, in a gym-slip. She had long red fingernails and she was singing to herself . . . *I live dangerous-ly, pom-pom; I live dan-ger-ous.* When I told her to get off the wall – from my bedroom window – she told me I was having kippers for breakfast.'

'Yes, she knows everything that goes on in the village.'

'Well, isn't it useful to a new school master?'

'Sure,' Peter took Tail's hand, 'that's why I'll have to marry you.'

Julia and I congratulated the two of them. Surprisingly Julia didn't ask when the wedding would be, and when I looked at Tony and Jill – sitting much too still on the hearth-rug – I understood why. Until the children's mother was well and able to settle with them in a new home, Tail and Peter wouldn't feel justified in leading their own lives.

Patch had given up wooing Biddy and was exploring the lounge. When Tail snatched the biscuits out of his way he lost interest in the lounge as well. He stood knocking on the door with his tail. When no one paid attention, he jumped at it until it opened a crack and then delicately hooked his paw round. A well-aimed push with his nose, and he was out. It had been an enchanting performance and the children were smiling with pride.

'Better find him,' said Peter.

'He can't get out,' Julia assured him. 'Don't worry.'

We forgot the little mongrel until we were ready to go down into the basement, but then the hunt was on. There was no sign of Patch in the kitchen or the living rooms, nor in the bedrooms upstairs. It was Tail who found him the second time round. Not much of him was visible; just one white fluffy ear and the eye with the black patch. He'd jumped on our bed, pawed back the cover and made himself comfortable between the sheets.

When Peter plucked him out, scolding, Patch went limp and cunningly snuggled against his sweater. I'd never seen a dog look so innocent and defenceless. He allowed Jill to put on his lead and trotted off behind her, tail and head down, dejection rather than protest in every line of his lithe little body.

The basement fascinated the children. There was a cabinet holding antiquated surgical instruments, a work-bench and shelves of tools, a rocking chair, a wine-rack full of bottles, a wooden rail of faded chenille curtains.

We were looking at the boiler when Patch gave a high bark and escaped Jill's hand. One moment I saw a field mouse swarm up the curtain, the next, Patch had sprung at it and brought it down with a well-aimed swipe of his paw.

'Get it!' screamed Jill. 'Uncle Peter . . . Uncle Peter! Don't let Patch kill it!'

Peter grabbed hold of Patch and I managed to catch the mouse. It was unhurt. Tail lifted the child in her arms and tried to comfort her.

Julia took the mouse and showed it to the child. 'Look Jill, it's all right. Shall we take it to the garden?'

'It's cold out.' The tears were still rolling down Jill's face. 'It's too cold.'

'I know where the nest is. It'll be warm in there. It's where the mouse belongs. Shall we take it home?'

The child nodded. Tail put her down and she followed Julia upstairs. Patch gave a sigh of contentment and stretched out on a square of old carpet.

Tony sat down beside the dog. 'Uncle Peter . . . Patch was just playing, wasn't he?'

'I think so.'

I believe the three of us had the same questions in our minds. How much had these children seen and understood when their father had been killed in Belfast? Would other youngsters have cared so much about the mouse?

Of course nothing was said and we made a job of lifting the heavy boiler into the middle of the floor.

'It's copper,' said Tail, 'like the three hundred pounds *antique* in Nether Craftly. Uncle Michael, do you think the sheep-dip will ruin it?'

'No, it's a beat-up old thing.' Big enough though to brew up a hundred gallons at a time.

'Wonder what it was used for,' said Peter.

'For washing clothes . . . things like white linen sheets,' Tail told him. 'My gran had one like that. We still have the big wooden spoon she used for fishing out whatever was in the boiler.'

'This one's been used once too often.' Peter had turned the boiler upside down and was running his fingers over the bottom. 'Mr Brogan should sell it to the antique shop. Someone might put plants in it and use it on the patio. All it's good for.'

Peter was right. The thick patina didn't entirely conceal the holes in the boiler.

CHAPTER 8

The owner of the patient wore a coat made up of so many silver foxes that I almost overlooked the patient – a very large and portly basset hound. Apart from the fox coat the tall, wide-shouldered man wore jeans and Texan boots made of thick hide.

He held out his hand. 'Glad to make your acquaintance Mr Morton.' The accent reminded me of what Tail had told me. Mr Fabricius was Craftly's only American resident, a sculptor of some renown, who was living in a luxurious caravan and working in a converted barn. Tail approved of him because he was spending much of his spare time constructing scenery for the Craftly theatre. 'My name's Fab . . . my hound's called Peabody of Flathanger.'

'What can I do for you, Mr Fab?'

'Just Fab . . . I guess I'm bothered about Peabody.'

'Why's that?'

'Look at my boots.'

Clearly Peabody had taken quite a few bites into the boots.

'I can't wear sneakers any more,' complained the basset's owner, 'because Peabody bites so it hurts.'

The dog looked anything but vicious. I offered him the back of my hand and he licked it. 'Does he bite other people?'

'No, just me. And only my legs . . . Watch!'

Fab picked up his dog by the front legs and lifted him above his head. The animal gave a squeak, trod air with the hindlegs and struggled to roll up into a ball.

'Come on, dance Peabody.' Fab laughed, 'Isn't it cute?'

'Cute!' I took the basset away from him. 'It's brutal.'

'Pardon me?'

'You're hurting the dog, picking him up like that.'

'Mr Morton, if you hadn't taken Peabody you'd have seen it all . . . When I put him down he hops around and snarls, and then he bares his teeth and goes for my legs. It's kinda sick.'

'It's very normal, Fab. How would you like to be strung up by your hands and made to dangle from a great height? Sheer torture. You might have dislocated Peabody's shoulders. Didn't they teach you anatomy at art school?'

'What's anatomy got to do with it?' he looked genuinely puzzled.

'Compared to his length and weight, your dog has very short legs. Don't you see? if you pick him up by the front legs you put an extremely painful strain on his shoulders.'

'Gee, you're right. I'm sorry . . . But why hasn't Peabody bitten my hands? Wouldn't it be more logical?'

'Maybe logical but not so good-natured.'

'He doesn't want to hurt me?'

'Apparently he doesn't, though you certainly don't deserve such consideration.'

'He's a great dog.' Fab looked downcast. 'When Peabody was a puppy he used to nip my hands sometimes . . . just when I was playing with him. I guess I yelled . . . so he does in fact know that it hurts. And he bit me only once when I had sneakers on and I didn't react. I guess it didn't bother me that much.'

'In these boots you feel nothing at all?'

'Right . . . I guess you've solved my problem.'

'I hope I've solved Peabody's problem.'

'Sure, Mr Morton. Poor old pooch . . . I'll never pick him up like that again. Can I settle your account right now?'

'I won't charge you. I haven't treated Peabody of Flathanger.'

'No,' Fab grinned. 'I guess it's me you treated . . . You can't be a dog psychologist.'

'I thought I've been using a little psychology.'

'You did. I was just thinking of the guy I took Peabody to in New York. He was a dog psychologist. He knocked my pooch out with pentothal – that's the truth-drug, I think.'

81

'What happened?'

'Peabody cried like a baby. So the guy said he was an unhappy dog, and maybe the breed was kinda miserable. And for that he charged me two hundred dollars . . . Say,' Fab groped in the pocket of his silver fox coat and brought out a brooch which looked like a miniature sculpture of two butterflies. 'How do you like it?'

'Very much.'

'Know what it is?' He pointed out the marks on the heads of the butterflies. 'It's a little head of your queen . . . the silver jubilee hallmark . . . I've been making these things as souvenirs. You have this one for your girl.'

'My girl's my wife. It's very generous of you.'

'Well . . . I kinda like working in siver now and then. It's a holiday from making big sculptures in copper and bronze. Right now I've got copper on my mind. Say, why don't we go downtown for a drink so I can consult you about it?'

As soon as we entered the Craftly Arms I knew that I shouldn't have agreed to going *downtown* with Fab. The first person I saw, sitting at a saloon bar table, was Dick Craven. He stared at Fab in his silver fox coat, and then bent down to pat Peabody.

'Don't often see bassets nowadays,' remarked his companion.

'He's from America,' said Craven.

That short exchange made Fab look extremely worried. 'Let's stay at the bar.' He chose a spot as far as possible from Craven's table. 'He's the ministry vet, isn't he?'

'Yes. So what?'

'See the guy with him? . . . Two pints of bitter, landlord . . . The tweeds the guy's wearing aren't fooling me, Mr Morton; he's an official . . . senior executive, I guess . . . could be from the home of the foreign office. Mr Morton, that guy's bothering me a whole lot.'

'I don't see why he should, whoever he is.'

'Because,' an ironic world-weary smile curved up Fab's lips, 'because I am conservationist. Maybe the public doesn't know me as a sculptor, but I'm sure known as a conservationist. I march, Mr Morton. In New York I march against the landing of Concorde. In Bonn, Germany, I marched on account of teachers getting sacked for their left-wing opinions . . . and in London I marched with the Popular Front against the Communists . . . and again in a protest against the cutting down of hedges. Mr Morton, I'm a marked man, and that guy with the ministry vet knows it.'

'You sure he isn't from the FBI?'

Fab was not amused. 'He could be. Sometimes our secret services work *with* the English, sometimes against them. Politics. It's all politics.'

'Look here, we're in an English village, in a quiet country pub. There's no great political conspiracy . . .'

'Can you prove it?' His feelings were so intense that a tremor agitated the hairs of his silver foxes. 'Remember what happened to my friend Adolf Apfelsauce!'

The name rang a bell, though not a loud one. the home secretary – or had it been the foreign secretary? – had decreed that Adolf Apfelsauce was not an asset to British security and should be sent home to America. Adolf Apfelsauce, who preferred living in London, had made a series of legal objections and appeals – at great expense to the British taxpayer. Nasty words, like dictatorship, had been bandied about and aroused the partisanship of the publicity-hungry and a lot of publicists. Meaningless words like liberty and democracy had been bandied about before Mr Apfelsauce had finally returned to his native land.

The silver fox coat trembled. 'You do know what I'm talking about, Mr Morton. As every fair-minded man must agree, the Apfelsauce case was a disgrace for your country and . . .'

'I'm reasonably fair-minded, Fab, and I don't agree. There's absolutely no reason why we should let every foreign national, who prefers to live in England rather than Japan, America or Timbuctoo, stay permanently or even for a day in our country, is there?'

Fab shook his head. 'I don't get you. You're saying these fascist-style things . . . and yet you're a nice guy; I mean

83

you were real kind to Peabody.'

'Your hound isn't a reformist, an anarchist or a conservationist . . . at least, not as far as I know.'

'I thought you were in favour of conservation. Tiger said you're with us.'

I got the message. 'I'm in favour of a *choice* of sheep-dips, especially dips that cause less pollution of soil and water.'

'I get you . . . you're an anti-pollutionist.'

'Fab, I'm not an *ist* of any kind. I just take things as they come. And that doesn't make me a *come-ist* either.'

We were finishing the beer when Dick Craven and the tweedy man came over to the bar. 'Nice dog.' Craven really was taken with Peabody. 'Wish my daughter could see him. She breeds dachshunds up in Yorkshire . . . By the way, this is Arnold Brownlow.'

'Fab shrank into his furs. 'From London.'

'That's right,' said Brownlow.

'Have a drink with us?' I asked. If Craven could play it bland, so could I.

'No way!' Fab grabbed my sleeve. 'We gotta go.'

'That guy might have been from the home office.' Fab was almost running through the lane, away from the pub.

'Perhaps you shouldn't have been so rude then.'

'Gee, I just wanted to get away.'

A few lazy snowflakes were drifting down, detergent white against the dirty grey sky. The light on the fields and downs looked dreary and cold.

'Listen,' Fab stopped so suddenly that Peabody had trouble putting on his brakes. 'I need your advice. Couldn't talk in front of those official guys.'

'But they *liked* your dog.'

'It isn't Peabody I wanna discuss . . . It's about the boiler.'

'The boiler for the sheep-dip?

'Right. The thing Tiger's trying to achieve is great. I'm with him . . . and with Tail and the others . . . one hundred per cent. Now . . . they need the boiler for cooking the dip. Right? And the boiler's got holes in the bottom. Right? Last night they tried to mend it. But you can't fill up holes and cracks with solder . . . it just runs over the place. The way to mend the boiler is . . . you cut pieces of copper the right gauge, then you shape them to lie flat over the holes and then you solder them on . . . and that's a skilled job.'

'So they've asked you to do it?'

'Right.'

'Then the problem's solved.'

'I'm one hundred per cent with them. I wanna do the job, believe me . . .'

'Whenever anyone says to me *believe me,* I don't. So why don't you want to mend the boiler?'

'On account of what happened to Adolf Apfelsauce . . . I can't work in New York. Back home my mind's a blank. Besides, I can't sell my sculptures in the States. I guess my designs are too European in character. You see I gotta live in England; it's essential.'

'You *are* living in England.'

'Right; so I can't afford committing an action that'll give them an excuse for expelling me.'

'Surely you don't think you'd be kicked out for mending the sheep-dip boiler!'

'Guess they could make it a reason . . . You saw the official guys right there . . .'

'A Ministry of Ag and Fish vet and a man from London– who could be anyone.'

'Yeah, he *could* be.'

'You don't want my advice,' I told Fab. 'You want me to give you an excuse for not mending the boiler.'

'You're wrong.' He looked so hurt that I felt sorry for him. 'I guess I want you to convince me that it's okay for me to do the job . . . Just one or two reasons why they *won't* throw me out the country.'

'You won't be committing a crime.'

'They could say I've done something that's against the ministry policy. Wouldn't that be treason?'

'No, not even an indictable offence . . . Anyway, you're

85

not involved in sheep-dipping policy. You're just helping a friend.'

'Maybe Apfelsauce was just helping a friend.'

'Certainly not a man like Tiger.'

'Is Tiger an okay person?'

'God! Tiger's a world-famous playwright.'

'Writers and artists – bar pop-singers – aren't popular.'

'Besides, Tiger's a viscount.'

'Hey! That's right! I'd forgotten. I guess even politicians wouldn't tangle with a member of the aristocracy.' Fab strolled on, almost relaxed. 'Maybe I'll do this thing for Tiger.'

'Just *may be*?'

'Wait a minute . . . Man, this is real heavy. It's blowing my mind . . . I gotta have some kinda security.'

'A certificate from the boiler-menders' union?'

'Man, I'm serious.'

'Well, I don't know what to suggest.'

'I know . . . Are you a certified veterinarian?'

'If you mean . . . am I on the register of veterinary surgeons? Of course I am.'

'So, if you did anything illegal you could be struck off?'

'Yes. But I don't see . . .'

'That makes you a member of a responsible profession. Okay. I will mend the boiler . . . on condition that you're present while I do the job.'

CHAPTER 9

From outside, Fab's workshop still looked like a sixteenth-century barn, but inside every conceivable fire-hazard – including most of the heavy roof timbers – had been covered with sheets of asbestos or metal. The precautions were sensible; there was a lot of dangerous equipment about, such as blow-torches and gas-cylinders. Fab obviously needed the stuff. His workshop was populated with enormous sculptures, unrecognizable and somewhat menacing shapes, though one bronze did look like a harassed version of the Loch Ness monster.

My father-in-law was gazing at the sheep-dip boiler, which was sitting upside down on fire-bricks. 'Never seen a tinkers' place like it,' he announced all too audibly.

'Daddy *please*,' pleaded Julia. 'Mr Fabricius is an artist . . . a sculpture, not a tinker.'

'Rubbish, girl! Tinker's job mending pots.'

'Mr Fabricius is an American and . . .'

'Yank, is he? Must say, I've never heard of a Yankee tinker before. Over there they don't go in for this sort of thing . . . too much money around in America.'

'Daddy, Mr Fabricius is an expatriate . . .'

'I dare say, a dedicated expatriate.'

Julia sighed. 'Dedicated to what?'

'To maintaining his expatriate status . . . what else? At times you're as dim as your late mother, Julia. You really should show more understanding for this poor foreign tinker. After all, we lived in India, Africa, Burma . . . Fact is, *we* were dedicated expatriates. Still would be, if that fellow Mountbatten hadn't given India away. I certainly didn't want to lose my expatriate status and return to Leamington Spa . . . I say, is that a bar over there?'

'Let's see.' Julia grabbed her father's arm and propelled

87

him to the trestle table at the far end of the workshop.

Fab had made sure that there would be plenty of witnesses when he mended the boiler. Tail, Peter and Bobby were setting up a buffet. Tony and Jill, with Patch, were watching Fab's preparations at his work-bench. Tiger was wandering from sculpture to sculpture, stroking his red beard like a prospective buyer, and Claire, wearing one of her lilac-pointed Siamese cats around her neck, was guarding the sculptures from the bulk of Bionic Baa. The big sheep had arrived with Claire and Tiger, in their landrover. According to my wife. Bionic Baa was like Queen Elizabeth I; but unlike the queen Baa didn't have the heart of a king but of a lap-dog.

'What's this? What's this?' Father-in-law was bending over the pot simmering on the gas ring.

'Something to keep us warm.' Claire picked the cat off her shoulder and deposited it on Bionic Baa's back. 'Not a punch, Colonel . . . something much more exciting. One of tiger's new recipes . . . onion-and-mint tea. Will you have a glass?'

'Oh . . . er . . . not just yet, thank you, dear lady. Might try one of these . . . er . . . biscuits though. What are they?'

'Japanese seaweed with grated acorns. Tiger adores them.'

Father-in-law withdrew his hand. 'Later perhaps. Think I'll see what the tinker fellow's doing.'

Jill presented her dog to Claire. 'This is Patch. What's the name of your cat?'

'Chiang-Ch'ing . . . She's called after the widow of Mao-tse-Tung. He was the Chinese leader.'

'Why did you call the cat after the widow?' asked Tony.

'We had to,' Claire told the children. 'You see, our first two cats were called Mao-tse-Tung and Chou-en-Lai.'

They obviously didn't see, but that didn't diminish their fascination with the cat which was fast asleep on the sheep's back. Thinking of my own boys, I had an idea how Tony and Jill felt; excited about being allowed to stay up late in an adult party, savouring everything unusual from the name of Claire's cat to Fab's activities at the work-bench.

Gradually we'd all gone to watch him beat pieces of copper to fit over the holes in the boiler. He was shaping more curves and dents than I'd have thought necessary, which entailed frequent heating with a blow-torch.

'Got to anneal your metal properly,' the colonel told Fab.

'Oh God!' whispered Julia. 'He's going to teach his granny to suck eggs.'

'Sure,' said Fab, gently, 'gotta anneal just right.'

'Learned a thing or two about metals when I was serving in Rawalpindi. Needed a lot of new equipment, transport . . . what have you; damned chairborne types in London kept ignoring our indents. Short of engineers too. Said to my chaps, *nothing for it. Patch up the stuff we've got, best we can . . .*'

'Daddy!' Julia shouted above the din of the hammering. 'Mrs Shrapnell . . .'

The colonel whipped round smartly. He scanned the workshop. 'Desirée? I can't see her.'

'Daddy, I was asking you whether she's coming.'

'No, 'fraid she couldn't make it. No baby-sitter for the dogs . . . Now, where was I? You know Julia, you're always interrupting. Just like your sainted mother . . . Ah yes, I was telling you about annealing. Did a bit myself, in fact. Thing is . . . when you beat metal it gets hard, so you've got to heat it frequently to make it flexible again.'

'Sure,' agreed Fab.

'Chaps make the mistake of not making it hot enough.'

'Right.' Fab was playing a strong flame on a piece of copper. When it turned red and almost transparent he switched off the torch, picked up the copper with tongs and dipped it in a bucket of water. The metal hissed like an angry snake.

My father-in-law shook his head. 'Not heated enough, if you ask me.'

Fab grinned. 'Well, sir, let's see whether I can get away with it.' He fished the copper out of the water, dried it on a rag and put it on a leather-covered cushion.

We all watched as he selected a ball pein hammer and took a few well-directed swipes at the metal. Under those powerful blows it altered and moved like a living thing.

Fab contemplated his handiwork, head on one side, and then took the shaped patch to the boiler. It completely covered the edge, fitting tightly over the damaged area. 'This is the worst part,' he told us, 'so what I'm gonna do is . . . patch it inside and out.'

'That should hold,' said the colonel, doubtfully.

'Okay sir. I'll take your advice and go right ahead.' He picked up a flat earthenware dish with a white cone inside, put in some water and rubbed the cone around the dish. Then he dipped in a brush and painted the thickened liquid on the damaged part of the boiler.

'What's he doing?' Tony asked the colonel.

'Way it works, you put on the liquid – flux that is. Now . . . see the little pieces of metal he's putting all round the hole? that's solder. Got to have flux and solder to melt together two pieces of copper . . . the patch and the boiler itself. Wouldn't work without flux or without solder. Y'see, now he's putting on the patch . . .'

'He *is* good with small children,' said Julia. 'When I see him like this . . .

'You wish he'd never go back to Leamington Spa.'

'Oh no, Michael! You know I'm fond of him, but we drive each other up the wall. I always know when he's furious with me . . . he always says I'm like my *sainted* mother. No . . . I just wish he'd have somebody . . . not just Biddy . . .'

'Well, there's Desirée.'

'Mrs Shrapnell? You can't be serious. She's twenty years younger than he. Can you see daddy with a strapping French woman who wears see-through shirts?'

'Oh, I can. You know, your daddy hasn't always been a father . . . not even a lousy one.'

Julia's grey bushbaby eyes went thoughtful. 'Michael, you don't think he's being serious?'

'No. He's on holiday. It's just a shipboard romance, I expect.'

'That's it. Daddy's generation used to have flirtations, whatever that was.'

'I think it was bedless fun.'

'Oh well . . . nothing to worry about then. I mean . . . I don't like daddy being all alone, but at his age . . .'

Age wasn't troubling the colonel. Between keeping the children interested with a running commentary on the work and telling the *tinker chap* how to do his job, the colonel soon appeared to be in charge of us and operations. That was probably the reason why the mending of the boiler took so long.

It was past midnight when Fab pronounced it free from leaks, and when Shorty arrived to take Bobby home and to let us know that the sheep-dipping problems weren't solved by any means. The man we'd met in the Craftly Arms with Dick Craven had been holding meetings at the veterinary investigation laboratories. In Shorty's opinion it meant that the *establishment* was taking counter-measures against the anti-BHC rebels.

Though I was tired after the boiler-mending party, I couldn't sleep. Half-seen images and vague impressions kept drifting through my mind, in some cases becoming sharper and more disturbing.

How were we going to cope with the colonel? In a week my work in Craftly would finish and we'd be going back to London. And father-in-law was still brushing aside any idea of returning to Leamington Spa. His sole concern was his animal; Biddy would fret if she were separated from Bachelor, and as Bachelor was a working collie there was no question – even if Tiger had been willing to part with his dog – of transplanting him to a town flat. Besides, Biddy was benefiting from country-life with her mate, learning sheepdog craft as well as roadsense. The colonel was infuriating Julia by telling her that he'd be perfectly all right in Craftly without us, totally ignoring the fact that Phil Brogan was entitled to getting nis house back free of our guests.

Then the children from Ulster, Jill's small face lit by the flame of the blow-torch and Tony cradling Patch in his arms so that Patch shouldn't be excluded from watching Fab's wizardry. The excitement of watching solid copper respond to the flame and turn into something as bright and changeable as fire and light. Strange that it had been Claire, with her cat and her sheep, who'd made them break their silence. I'd heard them tell her of their father's old car and how he'd built a new chassis for it in his workshop, how he'd made and welded the parts and made the sparks fly. They'd even spoken of their father's funeral; the arrival of Uncle Peter and Aunt Jenny, the hundreds at the graveside – mourners of the Women's Peace Movement. Suddenly, Patch squirming out of Tony's arms to lift a leg against the metal Loch Ness monster. And Fab saying not to worry, the little dog was only helping along the formation of patina on the sculpture.

Tiger studying Fab's weird sculptured giants and saying that his new play – in the light of what he was seeing – would have to be re-worked. *Psht* was wrong . . . dreadfully wrong. What had possessed him to make it a play without words? Words were essential in expressing total non-communication. But naturally all of them would have to be three-letter words. Tail, pleading with Tiger; *Psht* was perfect as it was. Besides it was scheduled for opening in three weeks. No time for changing the sets, the cast, the posters and just about everything else. Tiger thought *Psht* might be put on around the maypole on 1st May. At Christmas one could always put on *The Importance of Being Earnest*.

The trouble with Tiger was that one didn't suspect him of being practical and down-to-earth. And yet he'd made a fortune out of what most people would regard as unpromising and obscure plays, he was successfully running his home-farm – successfully, despite such employees as Masters and the Duke of Alanspring. And he was right about the potential dangers of the BHC sheep-dip too. All the same,

92

I wished it had been anyone but Tiger that challenged the bureaucrats with the alternative dips.

Shorty had established that Mr Brownlow, Dick Craven's pal from London, was in fact a man from the ministry. I didn't think his mission was to get Fab sent back to the States. Shorty had been convinced that Dick Craven, who had to live with the communities of Craftly and Nether Craftly, had sent for reinforcements from headquarters. Presumably Brownlow would be the arbiter in the sheep-dip situation. There was an uncomfortable question in my mind. Faced with Tiger and Claire – and, heaven forbid, Chiang-Ch'ing and Bionic Baa – how long would the man from the ministry remain impartial?

CHAPTER 10

I didn't know the farm I'd been asked to visit, but I recalled that Mr Standing was one of the small group who hadn't dipped his sheep yet and was waiting for Tiger's supplies.

Tollwood lay in a hollow, screened by sycamores and ash-trees on three sides. It didn't look good grazing land, more a place for small-scale mixed farming. On my way to the house I did in fact drive past poultry batteries, a small piggery and an ill-kempt paddock with a couple of muddy horses.

Standing, a man about forty with long greasy hair and a bald pate, asked me into the kitchen while he put on an old army coat. Trouble with his sheep, he told me, and could we go over to the barns in my car.

Signs of decay were all too obvious; broken fences which had been rotting on the ground for a long time, gaping holes in the roofs and windows without glass – badly patched with cardboard.

Standing stopped me at the largest of the low buildings. There was no need to ask questions; I could see the *trouble* the moment he opened the door. More than a hundred sheep were crammed together in the stinking airless build-ing and all one could hear were the sounds of coughing and laboured breathing. In the corner, behind the door, lay a dead animal, its ribs showing through the shorn coat. Nor were the live sheep any fatter.

Making my way among them, I noticed their running noses, but above all the suffering in their eyes. 'You shouldn't keep your sheep in such a badly ventilated building.' I told Standing.

'Nothing to do with you,' he muttered. 'You're a vet.'

It didn't seem the right moment for telling him that the unsuitable housing of animals aggravated or even caused disease. If I antagonized him too soon, he'd probably send me away and then blame me for the deaths of most of his animals.

'What did you do to their coats?' I asked. 'They haven't been shorn, have they?'

'No, we plucked them.' He looked slightly less agressive. 'In the summer . . . I gave them this new drug that makes the wool come off easy. It's quicker than shearing and you don't need skilled men to do it.'

'What drug was that?'

'Don't remember. It's something my brother uses in America. He sent it . . . name like cycle.'

'Cyclophosphamide?'

'Yeah, that's it.'

'I didn't think farmers were using it; not just yet.'

'My brother's in research.'

'Didn't he warn you that it would leave your sheep naked . . . unprotected against the cold?'

'He said it was up to me if I wanted to try it, and to keep the sheep in.'

'In the right kind of housing, perhaps.'

I examined about a dozen of those poor emaciated sheep. All of them had a temperature and their respiration was too fast. Some were coughing and most had a nasal discharge. I told Standing that his sheep were suffering from bronchitis.

'Money down the drain,' he grumbled. 'But if they need a dose give it them.'

'It's not that simple,' I told him. 'My guess is that they're suffering from a virus infection after a period of colds and chills . . . due to this bad housing. By now the cause of their condition is probably bacterial. If that's right then I should be giving them antibiotics and sulphonamides.'

'I said, go ahead.'

'It could be the wrong treatment. Bronchitis can be caused by worms . . . in which case I should be giving them a different drug, something like tetramisole injections. Why I'm telling you all this; I want the laboratory to tell me that caused the death of the sheep over there.'

95

'More money down the drain?'

'It'll cost you more if your animals don't get the correct treatment.'

'All right. Come back when you know what to do.'

'If I were you, I'd do a few things for these animals now, or there won't be any sheep left for treatment.'

He was worried at last. 'What do you want me to do then?'

'First of all put them in a better place. It's got to be clean. They need more room and more air. Have you got a better building?'

'There's the tyebarn . . . but that's full.'

'Let's have a look.'

The tyebarn was one of the better buildings, at least it was dry and weatherproof. No doubt that was his reason for keeping his feeding stuffs and farm machinery in it. I told him to clear it out, to transfer the sheep, clean their present quarters and then split the animals between both buildings. It was not ideal, but the best he could do for the moment.

Back at the house, I remembered how little time Standing had left for dipping his sheep. It seemed an added complication. I was by no means sure whether animals in such bad condition should be dipped. According to ministry advice, sheep were not to be dipped when hot, tired, wet, thirsty or full fed. How much less when running a temperature and suffering from bronchitis – whether due to a bacterial infection or worms. I reckoned that the dipping of the Standing sheep would have to be deferred; with ministry consent, of course. In any case I'd ask the advice of Masterson, my colleague at Nether Craftly, and have a word with the people at the vet investigation laboratory.

I asked Standing why he'd put off dipping his sheep. Did he have strong views about BHC?

'It's the paperwork I put off,' he admitted. 'How can you run a farm with all the forms and instructions pouring in all the time?'

'Some are necessary. You've got to protect farm animals against avoidable diseases.'

'Yeah . . . Well . . . I hadn't done anything about the dip. Then Tail came along and told me about BHC and that the St George Clemenses were going to find a cheaper dip. She said if I used it instead of BHC she'd organize the dipping for me. Well . . . I mean . . . if somebody else does the work, what do I care?'

Those miserable Standing sheep kept worrying me, so much so that I went back to Tollwood next day. If nothing else, the financial message had penetrated. Standing had carried out my instructions and the animals did have more room, more air and the soft food I'd suggested. I decided to anticipate the lab analysis and treated them with antibiotics.

In the late afternoon I went over to the laboratories at Nether Craftly. I don't have boundless faith in our postal delivery services and it seemed the fastest way of finding out the cause of death in Standing's flock.

'No sign of worms,' the pathologist assured me. He was a tall young Indian with a string of meaningful letters after his name, which was Prasad. 'By what you tell me I wouldn't treat the survivors with anthelmintics . . . though we'll do further tests if you want us to.'

'I'll take your advice,' I told him. 'I suspect you know more about sheep diseases than I do.'

'Oh yes, you're doing a locum for Phil Brogan. Awkward time just now, isn't it?'

'You're thinking of the BHC business?'

'Yes. It's an unpopular subject. Put the cat among the pigeons.'

'I don't see why.'

'You wouldn't, if you don't normally deal with farm animals. It's the old story. Administrators versus clinical people. Those who give treatment, concerned with the patients and the environment . . . that is, possible dangers to living things. Those who're supposed to run services, concerned with administrative tidiness and pretty statistics.'

'Does that go for Dick Craven?'

'He's not the worst. Decent chap with no more imagination or brains than is strictly necessary for running his job. Your Craftly eccentrics are giving him a headache.'

'What's he doing about it?' There was no doubt in my mind; in Prasad I'd found someone in sympathy with those who looked ahead, scientifically or imaginatively. I realized for the first time why Tiger and I understand one another.

'We've got a man from the ministry down here.'

'I know, but what can he do?'

'Insist on carrying out regulations to the letter.'

That was in line with the warning Dick Craven had given me. 'What does it really amount to?'

'Well . . . your anti-BHC friends had better make sure that their dip doesn't become too diluted.'

It was good advice. As the alternative dips were legal, Dick Craven had no means of stopping us from using them. But any deviation from the BHC routine was bound to give his department more work. If he succeeded in making it cumbersome and time-consuming for sheep owners to use the alternative dips they'd become more inclined to revert to BHC in the future; and so yet another chemical would be polluting our land unnecessarily.

No, there was nothing Craven & Co. could do except take frequent samples of the dip for lab analysis. Naturally the samples would be taken while the farmers were dipping the sheep – when a helper might be topping up the bath with more than the prescribed amount of water.

Prasad said, 'I expect our lab will be working overtime this week.'

I wasn't too bothered about the new complications. With a highly-qualified scientist and a diseases of animals inspector on our side my commitment to the anti-BHC people seemed more than ever justified.

Dick Craven was going to be hyper-strict, therefore we'd have to be prepared. Prasad had as good as advised us to carry out our tests on the strength of the dip in operation. We now wanted independent lab services on tap.

The fine Georgian village house, which was Dr Eller's residence and surgery, was brightly lit. The shadows of people, moving behind the curtains, suggested that there was a party on.

Dr Eller himself answered the doorbell and held out his hand to me. 'Glad you could come. Let me take your coat . . . We're in the conservatory . . .'

'I'm not a guest,' I told him. 'I wondered if you could spare me a few minutes . . .'

'Aren't you in the sheep-dip business?'

'Well, yes. That's what I want to discuss with you, if I may.'

'That's what they're discussing in there . . . Tiger and Claire, Tail and the rest of them.'

'They've asked you for laboratory facilities?' I thought it most unlikely, but in Craftly nothing seemed impossible.

'Lab facilities?' Dr Eller's pink face looked puzzled. 'We are hammering out what you might call a strategy. Who are you?'

'Michael Morton. I've been doing a locum for Phil Brogan.'

'Oh yes, I've heard of you. What's all this about lab-work?'

'You know that Tiger and a few others are going to use a non-BHC sheep-dip?'

'Certainly, and a good thing too.'

I told the doctor of my discussion at the veterinary lab and asked him whether the laboratory at the hospital would be prepared to test the sheep-dip for us. Nether Craftly Hospital was one of the few still in the hands of general practitioners and Dr Eller was the senior physician on the staff.

'See your point,' he said. 'It would be sensible to get independent analyses . . . in case there's any doubt about the formula of your dips . . . Can't give you a definite answer now – got to see the staff first – but I'm pretty sure they'll do the job. How's your sister? She still in Kenya?'

'It's Phil Brogan who has a sister in Kenya.'

'Charming girl, your sister. My wife's very fond of her . . . good little horticulturist. My wife says she grows runner beans fourteen inches long, and they're as tender as the small varieties. Remarkable! Come along now . . . while the punch is still hot.'

The punch was cold but the atmosphere in the big conservatory was tropical. Flowering geraniums and wisteria had taken over the walls and there were troughs full of orchids and carnations.

'They've all gone haywire,' Mrs Eller greeted me, 'all flowering at the wrong time. Even my poinsettias. They definitely shouldn't have come out until Christmas. It's quite turned me against certain chemical aids . . . Now, let me see, you're Phil Brogan's young brother, aren't you?'

'Just his locum, Mrs Eller.'

'Never mind. Do you know everyone here?'

I did. Tail and Peter, Claire and Tiger, Bobby Bowles and Shorty, my father-in-law and Mrs Shrapnell.

'We phoned you,' Tail told me, 'but Julia said she didn't know when you'd be home . . . We'll be dipping the sheep on Thursday and Friday, doing them all together in Dave's bath.'

'So the boiler's stood up to the brewing.'

'No problem. Everything's organized except the PR side. Tiger's taking care of that. He's called a press conference, and tomorrow a TV unit's coming down. It'll be a super demo.'

I didn't like the sound of it. 'What on earth for? Surely there's nothing to demonstrate against.'

'Don't you understand Uncle Michael! It's a prophylactic demo . . . I mean, you demonstrate anyway.'

'Whether anything's about to happen or not?'

'It isn't as vague as you think . . .'

Tiger's voice came booming across. 'So, actually, we're thinking of next year and the future. We'll make the whole country aware of the dangers of BHC. We'll inform the public of the alternative dips, which are a considerably lesser danger to plant and wildlife. And – incidentally –

we'll make it very difficult for any bureaucrat to say that our dips are not freely available or that they are too complicated to handle. Next year no farmer will have an excuse for not using our dips . . . Now, the route: we'll be marching from Nether Craftly church to the council offices . . . where we'll meet the TV unit.'

'Have you informed the police?' asked Shorty.

'Yes. Old Bunny – er – the chief constable and Sergeant Piper will be there . . . They're not expecting trouble. One other thing; we must be suitably dressed.'

'Darling, of course,' said Claire.

'What I mean darling,' Tiger lifted Chiang-Ch'ing off his wife's shoulder, 'not your full-length mink.'

'But Chiang-Ch'ing adores the mink when it's cold.'

'Better leave her at home, darling. And you, Tail . . .'

'I know . . . not my Wuthering Heights dress and poncho.'

'Good girl. You get the idea . . . tweeds and anoraks, sober and business-like. That goes for you too, Michael.'

'I always wear normal clothes,' I protested.

'Well, those yellow oilskins of yours make you look like that North Sea fishman on the cigarette packets.'

'They keep me dry.'

'None of us is going to worry about the weather tomorrow.'

'We'll go in your car, Jasper,' said Desirée Shrapnell to my father-in-law. 'Must keep our banners dry.'

There were almost as many banners as people in the car-park in front of the council offices. Some two hundred had been press-ganged to stand and drift before the TV cameras. Miss Phoebe Langor must have been busy painting and lettering those banners. The one that she and Prudence Blessum were supporting depicted a salmon pink pig lying on its side. It read *Death to careless Poisons. The Royal Pig Society.*

Preserve! Preserve! said Mrs Shrapnell's placard, *The Royal Rabbits Jubilee Society.* Father-in-law's board merely showed BHC crossed out and *Royal Fusiliers*. Tail was representing the *Craftly Royal Jubilee Theatre,* Claire the *Royal Siamese Cat Club,* Bobby the *Queen Elizabethan Country Women's Society,* Mrs Eller the *Royal Pure Foods Society* and the duke of Alanspring and Masters the *Royal Samarkand Goat Breeders' Association.* The most astonishing sight was Bionic Baa, following Claire like a dog, carrying a sandwich board *No to BHC! Don't fence me in!*

Tiger, his red beard above most heads, was everywhere...directing photographers, talking to journalists, handing out leaflets and lining up tame local MPs who were to address the crowd.

'Tiger's had a brilliant idea,' Claire told Julia and me. 'John . . . he's the MP for our area . . . is going to thank the Ministry of Ag and Fish men for giving us their assistance.'

'What assistance?'

'But that's the fabulous thing! He isn't going to say.'

'A mild form of blackmail?' Julia smiled.

'Yes . . . More or less, we scratch your back so it wouldn't be nice if you scratched our eyes out.' Claire drifted off, the big sheep at her heels.

'Does it sound such a brilliant idea to you?' I asked Julia.

'Oh, I expect Tiger's right – as usual.'

'He could be right if he were dealing with boy scouts; never with bureaucrats like Dick Craven.' I propelled Julia to the car. 'Let's go, I have to catch up on work.'

She turned and looked back at the crowd with their placards and banners. 'They really are amazing . . . a grey, miserable November morning and they've turned it into something like a country fair.'

'It won't serve any purpose . . . Perhaps a zany item on TV that might amuse a few city people . . .'

'I don't know. *Somebody* at the ministry will remember what it's been about.

Perhaps an ambitious office boy with ideas of changing the image of old ag and fish..'

'And he might manage it at that . . . Michael, I do hope

daddy won't catch cold and go back to London with us.'

We were about to get into the TR2 when Tail's Peter came driving at us. He jammed on his brakes within an inch of our car. 'Can you come right away . . . please. There's been an accident . . . He's hurt . . . He's been knocked down by a lorry . . .'

'Who?'

'Patch.'

CHAPTER 11

They had put the little mongrel on the operating table He was still lying on a cupboard door, presumably the makeshift stretcher, looking as lifeless as any dead animal I'd ever seen.

'I could feel his heart,' said Tail, tears coursing down her cheeks. 'He's alive, Uncle Michael . . . isn't he?'

Peter put an arm around her. 'He must be,' he muttered desperately.

'What happened?' For a moment I wanted to put off touching the dog. I was afriad of not being able to do anything. The thought of facing Tony and Jill, who had so recently lost their father, was unbearable. It was bad enough seeing the misery in the eyes of Tail and Peter.

He said, 'Jenny was taking him down the High Street . . . A lorry mounted the pavement. He was going too fast . . . I don't think he saw anything . . . He hit Patch side-on.'

'Your sister?'

'Not hurt . . . A neighbour's with her.'

'The children are at school?'

'Yes . . . They don't know.'

Still fearing the worst, I began to examine Patch. His heart *was* beating but his breathing was shallow and uneven. I was looking at the unconcious animal's head for signs of injury, when Patch opened his eyes. There was no trace of blood in them. He moved his leg and gave a whimper of pain. Clearly, both his right legs were broken.

Julia, already in gown and cap, was looking at me. I felt thankful that she was there. I'd worked with better trained assistants than Julia but none had ever achieved a greater degree of coordination.

'Anyone in the waiting room?' I asked her.

'Nothing urgent. Josephine's coping.'

'Set up an intravenous drip, will you.'

'You've done all you can,' she said to Tail and Peter. 'Better go home now . . . or back to work. I'll call you.'

'Can you tell us . . .' Tail touched the shivering dog.

'We'll deal with the fractures,' I told her. 'I don't know yet whether there are any other injuries . . . I'm hoping that there's no brain damage.'

'Thanks, Uncle Michael.' She took Peter by the hand. 'You must go back to the school. At least Patch is . . . awake.'

The x-rays showed nothing but a transverse fracture of the femur and a slightly oblique break in the humerus of the right front leg – not that it wasn't more than enough for any small animal. I began to feel more hopeful of saving the little mongrel. If there was no brain-damage and if none of the organs had been injured it was just possible that Patch would be walking again within three to five weeks.

The general anaesthetic didn't upset the dog. Clearly the impact which had broken the bones had been *clean* and sharp. I found no splinters, nor were the tissues around the breaks much damaged, which helped the appositioning of the bone. For the shaft of the femur I used a Kirschner-Ehmer splint, driving the transverse pins into the long bones on either side of the fracture and finally holding them in position with an external clamp.

For the front leg I used ordinary transverse pins, which I drove through the bone at right angles to its length. I'd performed similar operations often enough but I'd never been more conscious of the fragility of a small dog's bones.

'He won't be lame.' said Julia as I put on an adjustable metal splint to hold the pins in position.

'Don't make any promises. We can't be sure.'

'Patch is young.'

'That will help.'

With the dog ready for the recovery cage, I suddenly realized that it was afternoon and that the children would soon be returning from school. I wanted to keep Patch at least until the evening.

'What do you want me to tell Peter?' asked Julia.

'The children can't have Patch just yet. We won't know what his general condition is until he comes out of the anaesthetic. They'll have to know the truth.'

'Oh no!'

'Can you think of anything else?'

Julia shook her head.

'Peter needn't say anything to the children,' I suggested. 'He could bring them here, straight from school.'

'Yes,' Julia agreed. 'If they see him it won't be so bad.'

I didn't wait for Tony and Jill. Standing's sheep needed further treatment and I decided to go over to Tollwood and give them their sulphonmides.

The animals weren't much better but at least they looked more comfortable. Standing was making a real effort to save them and I reckoned he wouldn't lose more than two. He had also called Dick Craven who had agreed to give him extra time so that the sheep wouldn't have to be dipped until they were fit.

By the time I got back my family was in the living room, drinking after-dinner coffee, and the children had been and gone.

'They didn't say much,' Julia told me.

'Did you expect them to?'

'No. I asked them whether they'd like to come back when Patch is awake.'

'I hope that wasn't unwise.'

'There was nothing else I could do.'

Julia brought me a steak and kidney pie on a tray. The colonel was fast asleep in front of the TV, with Biddy snoring at his feet. I half watched a harrowing programme about marriage guidance, thanking my lucky stars for Julia – who could handle our precocious sons and me, her father up to a point, and the owners of a smashed-up little mongrel.

When I'd eaten we went across to the surgery and

recovery cages. Patch had eaten every scrap of the chopped chicken we'd left him and was standing up, wagging his tail. I opened the wire-door and watched him walk out, a little gingerly but full of confidence.

'Where are Tony and Jill? asked Julia.

The dog pricked up his fluffy ears and looked around. I carried him out and put him down on the grass beneath some rhododendrons – a favourite squatting place for the dogs that visited the surgery. He sniffed and after a while he tried to empty his bladder. Finding it hard to lift his fractured hindleg, he pawed the ground trying out each leg in turn and finally lifted his sound hindleg. I'd never been more pleased to see a dog perform that normal function. And then Patch rewarded me more. Drawing his front legs up to his chest, he splayed the hind ones, farted and produced a good well-formed turd.

'Isn't it beautiful!' Julia almost went on her knees.

'Well, Patch is functioning.'

'Oh Michael!' she hugged and kissed me, her tears smearing my face. 'He's going to be as good as new. Say it . . . say he's going to be all right.'

'All right . . . Give it a few weeks and he'll be as good as new.' I picked up the dog and carried him into the living room, putting him in front of the logfire.

Biddy, who had so pointedly ignored him in the past, wandered over, sniffed Patch and lay down beside him. In a lazy, condescending way she even gave his face a lick or two. Patch rolled over on his back, presented his throat and asked for more.

When Peter and the children arrived Patch scrabbled to his feet and went to greet them, tail wagging at full strength. They sat on the floor with him, stroking his ears, his belly, full of silent joy.

'Can we take him home?' asked Peter.

'Yes, but don't let him move too much for the next week or so.'

'How can one stop Patch?'

'I'll give you something to keep him quiet. Mix it in with

his food. Let him out into the garden to do his business, but no walks for as long as you can keep him still.'

The children had been listening to me. Tony asked, 'May I carry him home? I'm stronger than Jill.'

Julia picked Patch up and put him into the child's arms. 'Like this . . . put your hand on his chest. Yes, he looks comfortable.'

I hadn't been aware that the colonel was awake, but suddenly he was on his feet, taking off his sweater. 'There,' he draped it over Patch, 'Armed forces first-aid book . . . rule one . . . keep the patient warm.'

CHAPTER 12

Patch's accident may have had something to do with it, but I certainly enjoyed seeing the High Street jammed with heavy lorries and juggernauts. They were stuck because the whole village had been taken over by sheep. The animals were being driven, at a leisurely countryman's pace towards Dave Thornton's farm. The TR2 was small enough to get through, slowly but surely, behind the sheep.

Among the collies, doing a good job, I noticed Bachelor with my father-in-law's Alsatian bitch. Her mate appeared to have trained her remarkably well. I thought that the dogs were doing all the work when I saw Masters and the Duke of Alanspring, dressed in what looked like mediaeval smocks and deerstalkers.

'Ah, Morton,' the duke leaned into my car. 'Good turn-out, eh?'

'What's going on?'

'Another couple of farmers are going to use our dips, so now all the sheep are going to be done at Dave Thornton's.'

'Will there be enough dip?'

'Certainly. The ladies are working on it.'

The ladies were. At the piggery, which had belonged to Conny before she'd married Dave, about a dozen girls including Tail and Claire, were brewing in the boiler and filling up the drums. A tractor was standing by, presumably to take the drums to the dipping site.

I left my car at the farm house and followed the sound of sheep. I came upon the site at the furthest end of Dave's land. The layout was near perfect. The pens, already half-full of sheep, had smooth rails set inside the posts so that there was no danger of animals hurting themselves. They were well sheeted to keep the wind out. The races and sorting gates were well placed for efficiently handling the animals in and out of the bath. The bath itself was of the walk-in type which would take the sheep in down a ramp and out over an up-sloping ramp. A nearby stand-pipe showed that there was an adequate water supply.

Dave came to meet me. 'Want to have a look at my ram?'

'Thought I'd better.'

'He's over there, on his own.' He led me to an enclosure inside one of the pens.

Dave held the ram for me while I examined the place where he'd torn off his horn. The skin looked thin but the wound had healed perfectly and the animal seemed none the worse for its painful accident.

'It'll be all right to dip him,' I told Dave.

'Thanks. That'll save us a bit of trouble. We'll start dipping at seven tomorrow morning. Take a look round.'

Tiger was inside the shed beside the bath, counting drums of dip. 'We're all set,' he told me, 'except that some of the sheep are still missing.'

'They're on their way . . . Blocking the traffic in the High Street at the moment.'

'Good.' He looked through the door at the men who were wandering towards the bath. One of them was Dick Craven. 'We'll be well policed tomorrow. Shorty's been sent off to supervise dipping at the other end of Nether Craftly, and Craven's sending his new man here . . . fellow called Sears. Brownlow's at the laboratory, and – according to the bush-telegraph – three more men have booked in at the Craftly Arms.'

'You're not worried, are you?'

'Well,' Tiger contemplated the two men outside. 'We'll have to watch out. Can't afford a slip-up. You going to watch the show?

'I might even give you a hand.'

'Right. W'll have a set of protective clothing for you . . . in the shed here.'

'Don't forget Bionic Baa. Though you and Claire don't think of her as a sheep, she's got to be dipped too.'

'I say . . . that's true. Thanks for reminding me.'

Dick Craven caught up with me at my car. 'I hear you've arranged for your dip to be monitored at the hospital,' he said, not unpleasantly.

'*Your* dip . . . as approved by your ministry.'

'Quite . . . Aren't you people taking rather unusual- . . . precautions?'

'Just making sure that the dip's up to ministry specifications and standards.'

'I appreciate that.'

Driving back to the village I wondered how Dick Craven had meant it. *I appreciate that* is one of those ambiguous phrases which can mean *thank you* or *I know what you're up to*. I thought the latter was the more likely interpretation . . . not that we'd been up to anything worse than exercising our rights to making a choice. But then, nasty things were happening to democratic rights; our rulers were doing their damnedest to stop us sending our kids to schools of our choice, trying to stop us spending our money on private rooms in hospitals, making it less and less possible for us to do certain jobs without being members of a trades union, taking heavy taxes from cigarette smokers while hounding them for being smokers. Sure, Dick Craven hadn't been able to prevent us from obtaining the alternative sheep-dips but until we had official acknowledgement that the animals had been properly dipped we wouldn't be in the clear.

In the afternoon, Josephine and I worked through the pending tray, so as to give Phil Brogan a clear start on his return to the practice. Evening surgery was quiet; a poodle with a splinter in her paw, an old labrador needing treatment for mange and a cat for urticaria.

After dinner I walked down to School Cottage to take a look at Patch. As I watched the little mongrel get up from his place at the fire it crossed my mind that most pet dogs have better manners than people. They rarely fail to welcome visitors, or show their pleasure if it is a friend.

Patch walked slowly and – naturally – a little stiffly but there was no lameness. Peter, his sister told me, was helping Tail with the final preparations for the dipping and

111

the children were at the school rehearsing the Christmas concert. They'd gone out quite happily, confident that Patch was well enough to be left with their aunt.

'It was lucky that you were here to operate on Patch,' said Jenny. 'Phil Brogan wouldn't have managed it so well.'

'I think he would. He's got a good operating theatre and equipment.'

Jenny laughed, 'We call him the horse doctor. He's better with farm animals than pets.'

'And I have a lot to learn about farm animals.'

Jenny gave me father-in-law's sweater. 'Jill wants the book the colonel mentioned, for Christmas.'

'The armed forces first-aid book? I'm not sure there is such a thing.'

'We'll find it, whether it exists or not.'

'I'll ask my father-in-law to find it for you.'

I noticed the smell as soon as I entered the house, a stink somewhere between tomcat and cesspool. In the living room Julia was mending one of those thick woollen socks the colonel always wore, while the colonel – in his black Japanese outfit – was sitting cross-legged on the floor. The yoga exercise – or perhaps it was meditation – didn't seem to conflict with the tumbler of whisky in his hand. On the couch beside Julia sat a big red fox.

'Don't move so fast,' Julia hissed at me. 'You'll scare the poor dog.'

'God almighty! That's no dog!'

'It's a dog-fox. Think I don't know? Isn't he a pet?'

'Some pet. Where did you find him.'

'On our bed. Poor thing . . . it must be awfully cold outside.'

'How did you get him down here?'

'I just talked to him.'

I could see it; Julia on her knees before that brute, fussing over him, murmuring in the soft voice specially reserved for exotic animals and non-pets. 'He's got to go, Julia. He's stinking the house out.'

'Never mind . . . Animals don't really stink.'

'This one does.'

'He's settled down beautifully, Michael.'

'You're not taking him back to London.'

'Michael, he wouldn't have come if he didn't want to live with people.'

A thought crossed my mind. I approached the fox quietly and looked him over. Sure enough, there were places on his neck where the hair was shorter – a sure sign that he'd recently worn a collar.

'Custer!'

The fox looked up sharply. He didn't move, but his muscles tensed.

'Don't upset him,' said Julia.

'Listen, he's the fox I told you about . . . the one that poor devil of a policeman was supposed to train to dig up dead bodies. Custer's-last-stand, that's who he is.'

'You gave him something nasty . . .'

'To stop him biting his paw to shreds.'

'All right, Michael, but there's no need to be nasty to him now.'

'Darling, I just want him to go back to his natural habitat.'

'And kill a lot of chickens? It's irresponsible. As a vet you should know better.'

'I do.' When Julia took up the wildlife cudgels there was no point in arguing with her.

I went out and opened the back door. By the sound of it Hugo Lavinski had been right; a vixen was lurking somewhere in the yard, trying to reclaim her mixed-up mate. I went to the cloakroom and picked up a piece of scented soap.

Custer watched my return with alert eyes. He was still reluctant to move, but as I approached him and he picked up the scent of the soap he leaped off the couch and streaked through the door.

Julia too leaped to her feet. 'What did you do to him? The

poor thing! Go after him Michael! Go on!'

'He *wanted* to go, Julia.'

'You scared him off.'

'Didn't you hear?'

'What?'

'His mate was waiting for him out there.'

'You're making it up.'

'He isn't.' The colonel took a swig of whisky and shook his head a Julia. 'You're becoming more and more like your sainted mother, Julia. No sense . . . Young fox. Obviously he wants to be with his vixen.'

'There *is* no vixen, daddy.'

'Rubbish. Saw them both, yesterday . . . over at Desirée's place. Lying in wait for one of Desirée's rabbits. Tried to shoot the pests.'

'Well,' Julia squared up to her father. 'I'm glad you missed.'

'Would have been a miracle if I hadn't . . . it was pitch dark. Now look here, girl. Don't you bother your husband with that damned fox. He's got a hard day's work ahead of him.'

'What do you know about it.' Julia's temper was rising.

'Sheep-dipping tomorrow, isn't it.'

'That's got nothing to do with Michael.'

'Women,' the colonel downed the rest of his whisky. 'Been married to the chap ten years and still don't know how he ticks.'

When I got to the dipping site at eight next morning the men had already established a conveyer-belt system. Outside the pens, the Duke of Alanspring was directing the dogs – Bachelor, Biddy and another collie. Inside the pen nearest the bath Tiger and Dave were handling each sheep into the gateway. And on each side of the bath Farmer Bowles and another man were holding the sheep in the dip. Sears, the newly-imported diseases of animals inspector, was standing by the trough, stopwatch in hand. Just by looking at Sears I felt sure that he'd see to it that every

114

single sheep would stay immersed for the statutory minute and not a second less.

I went into the shed and put the protective boots, trousers and coat over my clothes. Then I went inside the pen with Tiger and Dave. It was where another pair of hands was most needed.

Almost every animal was, in the first place, taking evasive action – escaping into a corner, trying to make itself invisible within the flock and nimbly twisting out of our hands. They were heavy animals, and after an hour my muscles were beginning to ache. But then the sun came out and I forgot the pains.

The winter-black branches of sycamores and elm-trees made a fantastic pattern against the luminous sky, and the farm-buildings in the valley had the clear simplicity of a child's painting. It was one of those rare moments when I felt totally conscious of being a contented part of the living world. I watched with enormous pleasure the clever, gentle manoeuvres of the collies – flat on the ground while working out their strategy or veering from side to side, paws flying – seemingly not touching the ground. At lambing time a dog such as Bachelor was likely to run up to ninety miles a day; I reckoned he'd do almost as much by the time the dipping was done.

As the morning wore on individual sheep impressed their personality on me. Whoever had invented the myth that sheep were stupid? One only need to look into their eyes – those intelligent eyes full of an awareness that humans were too ignorant to fathom – to realize that the consciousness of animals was probably more highly developed than man's.

Around eleven the landrover came up, and Conny and Tail put up a trestle table with scalding coffee, sandwiches made of home-baked bread and jam tarts.

'Haven't you got any work to do?' Dave ribbed me.

'I've been working too hard; that's why I need a bit of exercise.'

'Better call it a day,' he advised me, 'or you'll be too stiff to move by tomorrow.'

Sears had put away his stopwatch and was warming his hands on the coffee mug. 'Do you think we'll be through before dark, Mr Thornton?'

'Should be. Anyway, *your* job will be finished.'

Masters, who had been topping up the bath, brought down half a dozen bottles of dip. 'They're ready for the laboratory, sir,' he told Tiger.

I offered to take them in on my way home.

'You're having your dip analyzed?' Sears seemed genuinely surprised.

'We have an arrangement,' said Tiger, with his inimitable vagueness. 'Got to keep a check on things, don't you know.'

The diseases of animals inspector clearly didn't know.

Conny gave me a lift down to my car. She said, 'I've baked a couple of loaves for you. If you're going back to town on Sunday you might liked to take sandwiches...I'll give them to you now.'

Outside her front door Bionic Baa was wandering around with one of the Siamese cats asleep on her back. In the kitchen, Claire was preparing the next meal for the men – stirring a large pot of soup.

While Conny wrapped the loaves in foil, I reminded Claire that Bionic Baa would have to be dipped like any other sheep.

'I know,' she said plaintively. 'Isn't it ghastly.'

'You don't want her to go down with sheep-scab, do you?'

'Oh, she'll be done. Tiger absolutely insists. Actually it's all organized. Baa will be bathed when all the sheep have been done. We'll take her straight home and I'll do her coat with my hair-dryer . . . I mean, we just can't let her stay wet; the cats wouldn't like it.'

'We'll be having supper at the pub tonight,' Conny told me. 'Join us? It'll be pork pies, flaming sausages and beer.'

Flaming sausages . . . a Craftly institution. Driving along the familiar lane I remembered the old fellow who'd invented that speciality. The doctor had given him a rub for his rheumatics, the old farm labourer had tasted it and discovered that it was pure alcohol. Strange, inventive character that he was, he'd put sausages into a cast iron frying pan, poured the rub over them and set it alight. The result had been very tasty.

The old fellow had long since died but Craftly, it seemed, was still celebrating achievements – such as dipping the sheep in a less poisonous brew – with flaming sausages.

'Here goes!'

Claire, Tail and Bobby approached the sausages with lighted wax tapers. Three columns of flames shot up and the bar rang with cheers.

The door opened, and Dick Craven looked in. 'Oh . . . I say! Is this a private party.'

'Oh no, come and join us,' said Tail.

'Awfully good of you, but I've got some chaps here.'

'We know,' Tail grinned. 'Commissars from the ministry, or the FBI. Bring them along.'

There was a peculiar expression on Craven's pokerface . . . something resembling amusement. 'Delighted to accept your kind invitation.'

'Don't seem like a good idea,' said Fab. 'It's been a real good party.'

'It'll go on being a good party,' Tail assured him.

Some ten minutes later the door opened. Dick Craven entered, with five other men . . . all in uniform, the uniform of scoutmasters. Their bare knees under the baggy shorts looked strangely white and vulnerable.

Claire, ever the experienced hostess, broke the silence. 'Do come and try our flamin' sausages . . . No, I'm not swearing, gentlemen . . . They're actually cooked in alcohol.'

'We'll just have these nice-looking biscuits,' said Craven. 'My friends here are stronger characters than I . . . They don't touch alcohol.'

'Good show.' Father-in-law grabbed a jug of water and filled some glasses. 'Down the hatch, gentlemen. Was a scout myself once . . . Service abroad changed all that.

Water's no use . . . one sweats it out. Got to have something with – er – more body . . .'

'What *are* you doing in this get-up?' I asked Craven.

'I suppose you've been too busy to read the local papers,'
he said. 'Or you'd have read that the International Scout
Masters Convention is taking place in Nether Craftly
. . . for the first time ever.'

'And you are . . .'

'One of the scout masters.' His cold grey eyes were
laughing at me. 'It was certainly one good reason why your
sheep-dip revolt interested me so much . . . And your role
in it, Morton. I thought you showed a good deal of
enterprise . . . A very strong element of the scout movement, enterprise.'

THE END

HUMOUR

0352   Star

300698	Woody Allen **GETTING EVEN**	50p*
398973	Alida Baxter **FLAT ON MY BACK**	50p
397187	**OUT ON MY EAR**	60p
397101	**UP TO MY NECK**	50p
397632	Les Dawson **THE SPY WHO CAME**	50p
397020	Alex Duncan **VETS IN THE BELFRY**	50p
398612	**IT'S A VET'S LIFE**	60p
398795	**THE VET HAS NINE LIVES**	50p
396245	David Dawson **VET IN DOWNLAND**	60p
397535	Stephen John **WHAT A WAY TO GO!** (see also Tandem General Fiction)	50p
397314	King Kong **MY SIDE**	60p
397780	Spike Milligan **THE GREAT McGONAGALL SCRAPBOOK**	75p
397527	Jack Millmay **REVELATIONS FROM THE RAG TRADE** (See also Tandem General Fiction)	50p
396237	Stanley Morgan **INSIDE ALBERT SHIFTY**	70p
398965	**RUSS TOBIN'S BEDSIDE GUIDE TO SMOOTHER SEDUCTION**	60p
397454	**SKY-JACKED**	60p
396954	Harry Secombe **GOON FOR LUNCH**	60p
396148	Keith Waterhouse **MONDAYS, THURSDAYS (NF)**	60p

0426   Tandem

158350	Tony Blackburn **A LAUGH IN EVERY POCKET**	40p
136616	**DARLING — YOU ARE A DEVIL!**	50p*
157710	Spike Milligan **THE BEDSIDE MILLIGAN**	35p
157982	**A BOOK OF BITS OR A BIT OF A BOOK**	35p
15827X	**A DUSTBIN OF MILLIGAN**	35p
158199	**THE LITTLE POT BOILER**	35p
158008	Spike Milligan & John Antrobus **THE BED-SITTING ROOM**	35p

*Not for sale in Canada.

GENERAL NON-FICTION

0426   Tandem

162560	Gerty Agoston **MY BED IS NOT FOR SLEEPING**	50p*
162641	**MY CARNAL CONFESSION**	50p*
175824	Nigel Balchin **THE BORGIA TESTAMENT**	60p
175905	**THE SMALL BACK ROOM**	60p
176030	**MINE OWN EXECUTIONER**	60p
176111	**A SORT OF TRAITORS**	60p
180593	Bill Bavin **THE DESTRUCTIVE VICE**	75p
152028	Aubrey Burgoyne **THE AMAZONS**	45p
163796	Catherine Cookson **THE GARMENT**	60p
163524	**HANNAH MASSEY**	60p
163605	**SLINKY JANE**	60p
162803	Jean Francis **COMING AGAIN**	45p*
151496	Joe Green **HOUSE OF PLEASURE**	50p*
165209	Brian Hayles **SPRING AT BROOKFIELD**	50p
172167	Harrison James **ABDUCTION**	50p*
135148	**COMING MY WAY?**	45p
150937	**HAVE IT YOUR WAY**	45p
045386	Olle Lansberg **DEAR JOHN**	40p
151577	Julie Lawrence **BLONDES DON'T HAVE ALL THE FUN!**	50p
16539X	Keith Miles **AMBRIDGE SUMMER**	50p
171446	Jack Millmay **REVELATIONS OF AN ART MASTER**	50p
16248X	Ingeborg Pertwee **TOGETHER**	50p
178815	Betty Smith **JOY IN THE MORNING**	70p*
179455	**MAGGIE: NOW**	75p*
178734	**TOMORROW WILL BE BETTER**	70p*
151224	Joannie Winters **HOUSE OF DESIRE**	50p

0446   Warner/Wyndham

597724	Alex Cord **SANDSONG**	60p†
799416	Annabel Erwin **LILIANE**	95p

*Not for sale in Canada

FILMS & TV

0352   Star

30006X	**THE MAKING OF KING KONG** B. Bahrenburg	60p*
398957	**THE MARRIAGE RING ("COUPLES")** Paddy Kitchen & Dulan Barber	60p⁻
397276	**MURDER BY DEATH** H. R. F. Keating	60p*
398825	**McCOY: THE BIG RIP-OFF** Sam Stewart	50p*
398035	**PAUL NEWMAN** Michael Kerbel	75p
397470	**ODE TO BILLY JOE** Herman Raucher	60p*
398191	**THE ROCKFORD FILES** Mike Jahn	50p*
397373	**THE SCARLET BUCCANEER** D. R. Benson	60p*
398442	**THE SIX MILLION DOLLAR MAN 3: THE RESCUE OF ATHENA ONE** Mike Jahn	45p*
398647	**THE SIX MILLION DOLLAR MAN 4: PILOT ERROR** Jay Barbree	50p*
396490	**SIX MILLION DOLLAR MAN 5: THE SECRET OF BIGFOOT** Mike Jahn	60p
396652	**SPACE 1999: (No. 2) MIND BREAKS OF SPACE** Michael Butterworth	60p
396660	**SPACE 1999 (No. 1) PLANETS OF PERIL** Michael Butterworth	60p
398531	**SPANISH FLY** Madelaine Duke	50p
398817	**SWITCH** Mike Jahn	50p*
398051	**THE ULTIMATE WARRIOR** Bill S. Ballinger	50p*

0426   Tandem

180240	**AT THE EARTH'S CORE** Edgar Rice Burroughs	50p
180321	**THE LAND THAT TIME FORGOT** Edgar Rice Burroughs	50p
164164	**LENNY** Valerie Kohler Smith	50p*
16184X	**ONEDIN LINE: THE HIGH SEAS** Cyril Abraham	60p
132661	**ONEDIN LINE: THE IRON SHIPS**	60p
168542	**SHAMPOO** Robert Alley	50p

*Not for sale in Canada.

READ MORE IN PUFFIN

For children of all ages, Puffin represents quality and variety – the very best in publishing today around the world.

For complete information about books available from Puffin – and Penguin – and how to order them, contact us at the appropriate address below. Please note that for copyright reasons the selection of books varies from country to country.

On the worldwide web: www.puffin.co.uk

In the United Kingdom: Please write to *Dept. EP, Penguin Books Ltd, Bath Road, Harmondsworth, West Drayton, Middlesex UB7 0DA*

In the United States: Please write to *Consumer Sales, Penguin USA, P.O. Box 999, Dept. 17109, Bergenfield, New Jersey 07621-0120.* VISA and MasterCard holders call 1-800-253-6476 to order Penguin titles

In Canada: Please write to *Penguin Books Canada Ltd, 10 Alcorn Avenue, Suite 300, Toronto, Ontario M4V 3B2*

In Australia: Please write to *Penguin Books Australia Ltd, P.O. Box 257, Ringwood, Victoria 3134*

In New Zealand: Please write to *Penguin Books (NZ) Ltd, Private Bag 102902, North Shore Mail Centre, Auckland 10*

In India: Please write to *Penguin Books India Pvt Ltd, 706 Eros Apartments, 56 Nehru Place, New Delhi 110 019*

In the Netherlands: Please write to *Penguin Books Netherlands bv, Postbus 3507, NL-1001 AH Amsterdam*

In Germany: Please write to *Penguin Books Deutschland GmbH, Metzlerstrasse 26, 60594 Frankfurt am Main*

In Spain: Please write to *Penguin Books S. A., Bravo Murillo 19, 1° B, 28015 Madrid*

In Italy: Please write to *Penguin Italia s.r.l., Via Felice Casati 20, I–20124 Milano*

In France: Please write to *Penguin France S. A., 17 rue Lejeune, F–31000 Toulouse*

In Japan: Please write to *Penguin Books Japan, Ishikiribashi Building, 2–5–4, Suido, Bunkyo-ku, Tokyo 112*

In South Africa: Please write to *Longman Penguin Southern Africa (Pty) Ltd, Private Bag X08, Bertsham 2013*

Also by Helen Cresswell

THE NIGHT-WATCHMEN

The two men in the park look and live like
tramps, though they call themselves night-
watchmen, but whatever they are Henry
knows he will have to discover more about
their strange, secret life or die of curiosity.